I0592871

FILIGREE RINGS

(and other Fae things)

R.M.SELG

Book One of the Filigree and Fire Series

This is a work of fiction. Names, characters, businesses, places, events and incidents are either the products of the author's imagination or used in a fictitious manner. Any resemblance to actual persons, living or dead, or actual events is purely coincidental.

Version 1.02

Copyright © 2017 R.M.Selg

All rights reserved.

No part of this book may be reproduced or transmitted in any form or by any means, electronic or mechanical, including photocopying, recording or by any information storage and retrieval system, without written permission from the author.

Cover illustrations, design and book design copyright © 2017 R.M.Selg
Editing by K.A.Editing

Kalmus Publishing, PO Box 459, Mitchell ACT 2911, Australia

ISBN: 978-0-9876374-0-6

www.rmselg.com

For Wendy.

Always…

ACKNOWLEDGMENTS

I would like to thank everyone who has assisted me to complete this novel. Particular thanks go to my family and friends for their ongoing encouragement, support and proof reading abilities, including Linda Reid, Stephen Esdaile, Katrina Wunsch, the two de Gruchys, and Kath Read.

I would also like to thank Steven Lewis of Taleist, Joanna Penn of the Creative Penn and Nick Stephenson of Your First 10,000 Readers for passing on their knowledge of Indie publishing and marketing through their online training courses.

It would be remiss of me not to mention all the writers in the 10K Readers Facebook Group and thank them for sharing their experiences, expertise and enthusiasm. It is so nice to know you are not alone on your journey.

In the Beginning

Pain.

She was encased in a red cocoon of pain.

It was eating into her soul, her mind. There was nothing but intense, unrelenting pain. She was going to go mad.

Then it came; a tiny black piece of nothing.

She focused on it and it started to grow. Slowly it became walls of blackness and the red glow started to diminish.

Now there was just a small point of red light.

Now she was dissolving into nothing—the blackness was embracing her.

She opened her eyes for just a moment and saw a beetle flying above her; its wings shimmering green. It was so beautiful, that for a moment, she smiled.

Then her mind gave way and she lapsed back into darkness.

He didn't come this way very often, it was the long way home, but tonight he needed some fresh air. He had been having bad dreams again. Maybe the exercise would help him sleep. The bottle under his arm might help too.

It was late and the streets were dark. The council hadn't bothered with street lights in this industrial precinct. The night was warm, but every now and then a cool breeze would drift over his arms causing the hairs to stand on end.

Half way up the lane, he saw three shadows emerge from a warehouse, and instinctively he pulled into a doorway to avoid being seen.

The first two climbed quickly into a car. The third rearranged his hold on something and then awkwardly flopped into the front passenger seat.

The car drove away slowly; headlights off until it reached the intersection with the main road.

His heartbeat slowly returned to normal. He was an old man now. One of his friends had been mugged recently, and he had no desire to suffer the same fate. As he moved along the lane he noticed that the door to the warehouse had been left open. It was banging in the breeze.

Bloody thieves.

He peered inside, but it was too dark to see anything clearly. There was something dark on the floor. Then the smell came creeping into his nostrils. A veteran of the bloodiest battlefields in the world, it was a smell that still filled his nightmares.

The small torch on his keyring lit up her glazed eyes, a sea of red, and torn flesh.

He had to be sure; he moved a little closer…
Yes, she was definitely dead.

The old man skirted the lake of blood and fled.

It seemed like forever, but it was only hours later, that she awoke to brilliant sunshine shining through a skylight high above her. She had a faint awareness that she had felt incredible pain, but had no recollection of why. She was lying in an enormous old warehouse.

The blood around her was starting to congeal. She lifted her fingers from the puddle in which she lay, mildly fascinated by the feeling. It was like half-set jelly. She knew she should be frightened; that she should be in pain and she should be fleeing; but the numbness, the lovely nothingness, still had its warm fingers around her mind.

She stood up—moving slowly as if in a trance—the blood squishing up between her toes. Her right side was cloaked in red. She was naked. She had no wounds. She had no pain. She stepped into a shaft of sunlight and felt its warmth on her skin. She stared into the light. Something was wrong. She knew inside that she should be dead. Yet here she was. There was no body on the ground, no angels, no path of white light, and no heaven calling to her. She was here. She looked at her hands and touched her body. She was here; she was flesh; she was real.

She caught her reflection in a shard of glass.

This must be a dream—it had to be.

She had wings…

…but she was no angel.

The wings were dark green with strange black twisted markings all over them. When the light caught them, they shone; opalescent. They were jagged looking—like demon wings—and had a strange green glow to them.

She felt as if she would faint; her head was swimming.

Then she noticed the proportion of her surroundings. The ceiling was miles away and the door was the size of a sky scraper. Was this a giant's warehouse—or was she the size of a fly? The floor seemed to go on forever. Was this hell?

Then she saw the Christmas beetles. They were everywhere; their green and brown and pink hued shells wandering drunkenly around the floor. They were as big as boar hounds.

She heard a scuffle and turned to see two eyes glinting from under a stack of wooden crates. The rat crept forward, attracted by the smell of the blood. It was the size of a mammoth. Its nose twitched and it moved closer—she fled; running out through a hole in the wall and into the street.

The street was just as big; a nightmare of concrete and bitumen, steel and glass towering beyond the limit of her senses. She ran and ran until she could run no further. It had to be a dream. If only she could shake herself awake.

She slipped into another giant building, some kind of workshop, and hid behind some giant crates. She lay, curled into a ball, trembling.

He was running late, and there were no god damn parking spots anywhere. By the time he got to the café it was after twelve and he was almost an hour late. He had tried to call a couple of times but it had gone straight to her voice mail. Why would she have her bloody phone off? If someone was late, you'd keep the damn thing on. Maybe she was too busy yacking to someone to take the call.

There was no sign of her in the café. He ordered a coffee and sat down. Perhaps she was in the bathroom.

He didn't have time for this shit. The coffee arrived and he started to drink it quickly, wincing at the heat of it.

She must have left already. She was too bloody high maintenance, and the stupid bitch just didn't realise how important his work was.

He tried calling her mobile again, but there was still no answer, so he sent her a quick SMS—Where R U? Been waiting for ages.

He finished his coffee and went back to work.

Later that afternoon he tried calling her again. Still no luck. He hadn't received any response to his text either.

He dropped past her flat on the way home from work, but there was no answer. He gave up and went home.

The real estate agent parked his car and climbed out. He had a potential tenant coming to see the warehouse tomorrow, and he wanted to make sure it was immaculate. First impression was good—no graffiti outside or broken windows. He walked over to the roller doors—they were good too. He moved around to the side entrance and stopped. There were dark red footprints leading out of the door. Blood? The lock had been jimmied. He didn't like the look of it. He pulled a clean handkerchief out of his pocket and used it to gently push the door fully open. A rush of flies hit him in the face. The smell was awful. He quickly raised the handkerchief to his cover his nose and mouth, retching violently. One quick glance was enough. He called the police.

Rebecca

The bottle was tucked inside a brown paper bag and clutched tightly in his hand. He was still a bit shaky and he was worried he might drop it. He was not going to go back into the warehouse, but he had to see what was going on.

He couldn't go very far along the lane—there was a police barricade. A neatly dressed woman was questioning a police officer; recording it all on a small voice recorder. There were a few locals listening in. He spotted one that he knew and headed towards him rather than the police line.

'What gives?' he asked.

'Murder. Forensics all over the place. They haven't brought out the body yet.'

'Keep your eyes and ears open Bruce. I want all the gossip on pub night, OK?'

'Righty-o, Andy.'

He wandered away from Bruce and then sidled a little closer to the police line to try and hear the interview.

'We can't say at this stage, I'm afraid,' the policeman said.

'You can't even tell me if it is a male or a female? Is the body that decomposed?'

'I'm sorry, you have misunderstood me. There is no body. Just blood. At this stage, we cannot say whether the blood is human, so it is impossible to say if there has been a murder.'

'Okay, but based on your years of experience, what do you think we have here?'

'My years of experience tell me not to take a guess until the results come back from forensics, but we will be treating the matter with the same priority as a homicide for the time being.'

What had happened to her body? Maybe they had come back and moved it. Jesus, what if they had come back while he was there? He was starting to shake again.

Bugger. One of the cops had noticed him. He pretended not to notice the attention and hobbled back down the road. As soon as he turned the corner he broke into a shuffling run. He turned down another lane and backtracked a bit back towards the crime scene before entering a workshop via a loose bit of corrugated iron. He crept into a corner and tried to slow his breathing. He needed to be quiet.

It wasn't long before he heard them go past. They would give up soon, but they would probably put a description out to all the police stations in the area. The buggers would plague him until he spoke to them. Well, he would do so in his own good time. And not to just any copper either—too many bad eggs around here.

He pulled out the bottle. God he wanted it today. The nightmares had been terrible. And now the bastard things were pulling up other nightmares to join them. The dreams of Nancy were back too. He took a long swig and glanced up at the roof. There was a hole up there somewhere letting in a pinpoint of light. It was funny how the atmosphere in here actually made the light look green.

The light moved. A tree outside must be moving in the breeze; giving the light a green colour and making it waver. It moved again. He stopped the bottle an inch from his lips. The green light was moving directly along the beam above him. He got the distinct impression that it was trying to get away from him. He put the bottle down and stood up to get a closer look.

'Well I'll be blowed!' he whispered, 'I haven't seen one of you lot in ten years,' he said as he took a step backwards. Then suddenly his expression changed.

'Lucy?' he asked, lips quivering. 'Is that you Lucy?' He took a step forward, getting a good look at her.

'No. You...

'You're the lady from...' he said, completely at a loss.

'How can that be?' He stared at her, completely confused, she didn't reply.

'Do the others know about you?' he asked, suddenly concerned.

Her head cocked to one side.

'You haven't seen any others yet?' he detected a head shake.

'You can't stay here. There are coppers all over the place. If they find you, there will be hell to pay,' he took a cautious step forward, not wanting to scare her, 'and if the others find you, your life won't be worth living.

'Come on—fly down and hide in my pocket and I'll get you out of here.' The little fleck of green light grew agitated. He couldn't hear her words, but he could clearly hear the note of panic.

'You can't fly?!' he exclaimed, surprised, 'okay here, climb on my hand,' he said stretching as far as he could. She jumped onto his hand.

'In you go. Okay? Keep your head down! You're putting out quite a glow. My place isn't far. You'll be safe there until we work out what to do.'

He listened carefully at the wall then slipped out into the alley.

The bottle sat where he had left it, completely forgotten.

Homicide had been called to oversee the processing of the crime scene. Detective Inspector Tom Hayes was slouched against the wall, avoiding the flies and keeping out of the way while the forensic team photographed and processed the site. He was taking in the surroundings; noting the splatters and patterns of the blood and scanning the site for evidence. He was a tall man with broad shoulders and dark brownish red hair. His blue eyes could be startling at first glance.

It wasn't a murder investigation yet, but he was pretty sure it would be. The uniforms that had been called to the scene had alerted him, and they had done a nice job keeping the sightseers out and the crime scene clean. He hadn't worked with constables Gardiner and Peale before, but he had asked around and they had a good reputation.

It was Constable Ivan Peale that had spotted the old man nosing about outside and had discretely pointed him out, but Sergeant Howe had sent the two laziest uniforms he had after him. Of course he got away. The old bloke knew something. Tom had tried questioning another man that the old guy had been talking to, but didn't get anywhere. He had taken down his name and address and that of several other onlookers who were a little too interested in what was going on. He was pretty sure they were all rubberneckers rather than criminals returning to the scene of the crime, but it paid to keep an open mind.

Technically, it wasn't his case yet. As soon as the blood was identified as human it would be though. Not much he could do until then except keep his eyes and ears open.

As soon as the last customer for the day had picked up his car, they closed the roller door and collapsed at the table. The garage was large and old, situated in a run-down industrial area. It had once been a small-scale meat-works in the days when everything was handmade locally. No one paid much attention to their neighbours around here. That suited them fine.

The tall quiet one grabbed three beers from the fridge. The jumpy aggressive one sat chewing his greasy fingernails and the bald man sighed and sunk his head into his hands.

'What an absolute cock up,' he said in a muffled voice.

'No shit, Einstein,' said the finger-nail chewer as the tall one handed out the beers.

'Do you think it's true?' asked baldy, raising his head to face the tall one, the brains of the group.

'Dunno. Could be. Bloody weird if it is. Maybe some necro took off with her. The boss will find out. He's got a man on the force. For now, we just gotta keep our noses clean and keep everything quiet,' he said looking towards the old meat safe.

'Yeah right,' said baldy sourly, 'how much longer is that gunna be? I mean this is one red-hot potato.'

'I don't like it either—something's up. He should have been here by now,' said Jumpy, getting agitated again.

'Look if you're so bloody worried you go and talk to the boss,' said brains.

'No. You're right. We can wait. He's pissed-off-to-the-max as it is. The guy will come. We can wait,' and he went back to chewing his nails.

Once they were inside, he retrieved a clean handkerchief for her to use as a covering.

'I dare say you'd appreciate a bath. Can you make yourself bigger?' She shook her head. 'Hmm. Let's see what we can do then.' He rummaged about in the kitchen cupboard until he found an old sweet tin. It was half as tall as she was. He half filled it with warm water and placed a matchbox next to it as a makeshift step. He passed her another handkerchief to use as a towel, and a sliver of soap, sliced from the edge of a full-sized bar. An open recipe book standing on its edges served as a privacy screen for her.

He busied himself with the kettle at the other end of the kitchen.

The water was divine. The tin was a swimming pool to her and she completely submerged herself, wanting to wash away everything that had happened. The trouble was, she had no idea what had happened. She surfaced, the water turning red around her as the blood flowed off her skin and fanned out into the water. She could see her reflection in the stainless-steel toaster. What on earth was she? She tugged on her wings and was surprised to find that it hurt. They were definitely attached to her, a part of her, yet they felt alien to her, as though someone had been performing bizarre experiments on her.

She washed thoroughly with the soap, wanting to be free of the bloodstains. Eventually she was satisfied and clambered over the edge of the tin back onto the bench. Once she was dried and wrapped again in the other handkerchief she emerged from her enclosure and walked towards her rescuer. Who was he? How did he know about her kind—whatever she was? He was sitting drinking tea and reading a newspaper and it took a moment for her to get his attention.

'Feeling better?' he asked, when he noticed her. 'How about I bring you over to the table so we can talk?'

She nodded.

He held out his hand and she walked onto it. He turned and placed his hand on the dining table to allow her to step off.

'You could do with a seat,' he said and rummaged through his cupboards again.

He returned with a new dish washing sponge. She sank into it gratefully, it was surprisingly comfortable.

'Right. Now tea.'

She started to take in her surroundings. They were in an old terrace house on the edge of the industrial precinct. The kitchen was a mess of dirty pots and pans and the bin was overflowing with empty bottles. He had already apologised gruffly for the mess—didn't get many visitors these days. The table itself was clean enough, and so was the small lounge off to the side.

Before he had found her, she had hidden in a corner of the old workshop, trying to shake off the nightmare. She had panicked, she had recovered, and then she had panicked again when the old man had found her. She was starting to calm down a bit now, and the knowledge that a cup of hot tea was on its way was helping the stress to drain away. Hers came in a bottle top from a Tabasco sauce bottle and, thankfully, it had been well washed.

'Where did you come from?' he asked, leaning down so he could hear her better.

'I don't know,' she squeaked.

'You don't remember anything?'

'No; nothing since this morning—when I woke up in a pool of blood in a warehouse…with…with WINGS!'

'You don't think you had wings before?'

'No.'

He looked at her puzzled.

'Here I am and I can't remember my name, or where I live, or how old I am, or…

…or anything!' She was getting panicky again.

'Don't worry, don't worry! You've obviously had a bit of a shock. It's too early. You've got to give yourself some time. It will all come back eventually. You're safe here.'

'Where am I?'

'This is my house; we're not far from the Sydney Fish Market. For now, we have keep you safe. If the wrong people find out about you, you'll end up stuck in a cage in the name of science. I need to teach you how to look like a normal human being, so you can hide in the crowd—so to speak.'

'But I'm tiny!' she squeaked.

'Yes, that is the first thing we need to do. Teach you how to assume human size,' he said, sipping his tea, 'and it will make it easier to talk. I know you can't remember your own life, but do you know if you ever learned any tricks of the Sidhe?'

'Of the "she"? What's the "she"?'

'It's Celtic. Spelt S-I-D-H-E. Means the good ones, the lordly ones, you know—faeries.'

'I'm a fairy? How can I be a fairy? I don't even believe in fairies—fairies don't exist—how can I be something that I don't believe in? I can't remember anything, but I am sure in my bones I was a normal woman yesterday.'

'Well, I've never heard of a woman becoming a faerie, but I don't know everything there is to know.'

'But fairies are kiddie stories. If fairies are real, why doesn't everybody know about them?'

'Because faeries don't want you to know about them. Think of all the different cultures that have fairy stories—there are hundreds. Just because they are stories doesn't mean that they aren't true as well—or at least partly true. And even you must know how stories are gilded and exaggerated as they are handed down from parent to child.'

'Why haven't scientists discovered fairies then?'

'Because faeries have been lucky; because scientists would be mocked for working on faeries, and because faeries have some natural protections to keep them hidden. But every now and then, things get hairy and something almost comes out. Take the Cottingley fairy photos for instance. Faeries didn't understand what photos were at the time. When they realised what was happening, they had to magically change the negatives to make it look like they were just paper cut-outs. When the girls grew up and realised what they had done, and the danger they had put faeries in, they eventually "admitted" that the photos were a hoax. It was sad that so many people were made to look like fools, but a whole species was at risk—it had to be done.'

'You're telling me that the Cottingley fairies were real too!'

'Yep. It's going to take time to get used to this,' he paused and sipped his tea, 'you aren't what you were,' he said and shook his head, eyeing her curiously. 'You're a faerie all right, only God knows how it happened, and you don't know jack about being one. Lucky for you, I can teach you some of that. Nancy, my Nancy, she was one,' he said quietly.

'Your wife?'

'Aye. Almost fifty years we were a team.' He shook himself.

'We've got a lot of work to do. Do you remember if you ever learnt another language, especially any of the Celtic ones? You know, Gaelic—Welsh at a pinch?'

'No.'

'Damn. This won't be easy then,' he said getting up and pacing the floor. He came to a halt, 'okay—start at the beginning. Some stuff faeries do, they do because it comes natural—like learning to walk is to us. Flying is one of them. You are going to have to feel how to use the muscles in your wings and practise until you get it right. I can't teach you anything about flying,' he said, giving a dismissive wave, 'there are a few other talents you'll discover along the way that are just like that too.

'Then there are the magicks. This is where it gets harder and you have to know how to say the words properly in the faerie tongue. A lot of it is sorta like Irish but not quite—some of the sounds are similar.'

'How am I going to remember all this?' she said in a concerned voice.

'Don't worry, we'll do it a little bit at a time and keep practising until you get it right.

'Okay. To get to normal size—well human size—you have to say

"Moarh". And at the same time you have to think about being the size you want to be.'

'Moarh?'

'Yep—now really concentrate and try again.'

'Moarh' she said, screwing her eyes closed. Nothing happened.

'I would have been surprised if you'd got it the first time. Now—try again but this time, try to picture yourself next to something in the room,' he said, gazing around the room, 'say the chair—and you're gettin' bigger and it's gettin' smaller. Oh, before you do—we'd better put you on the floor.' He gently picked her up and set her down on the floor.

She did as he suggested, and this time, when she opened her eyes she was only slightly shorter than he was. Thankfully the handkerchief had increased in size proportionally.

'Ahh, that's going to make things much easier. But before you get too cocky, we need to make sure you can do it again. So—same principle but new word "Be-awgh" to get you small again.

'Be-awgh,' this time it worked first time. She was back to miniature.

'Okay, now back to full size again—this time—keep your eyes open if you can. It's safer.'

'Moragh,' she said. But nothing happened.

'Ahh, mucked it up didn't you? "Moarh" and "Be-awgh". It's gunna be hard to remember but you are going to have to learn it,' he said leaning down.

'Do all fairies speak this language?'

'I don't know,' he said and paused in thought. 'I suppose they must or they wouldn't be able to do the magicks. Okay—try again.'

'Moarh,' and she was back to his size again, what's more, she had managed to do it with her eyes open, even though it made her feel nauseous.

'Let me find some paper—you'll have to study this stuff and learn it by heart,' he disappeared down the hall.

Some of her fear was starting to fade. Maybe should could cope with this after all. She felt closer to normal being this size, the size she was accustomed to. It made the whole experience less surreal.

He returned a few minutes later with a pad of paper, a pen, and an old dressing gown. She slipped the gown on over her covering and tied it tightly at the front. She sat down at the table and wrote the words phonetically so she would be able to read them again later.

He made her a larger cup of tea.

Philip Cole tried to ring his estranged wife again. No answer. Still no response to his text either. He went past her flat on the way to work, but the car was not in its usual spot and there was no answer at the door. He needed some answers now goddammit! He drove to work.

A short time later he climbed the stairs to the building and pushed open the front door. His secretary was already at work at her desk and he nodded to her as he walked past and entered his office. He slipped his coat off and hung it on the rack then collapsed into his chair. The last month had been one shit fight after another, and he was completely over it. He pulled a thick wad of papers from his brief case as Vivienne walked in with his morning coffee.

'Take care of those will you,' he said pushing the papers into her hands. She looked them over; frowning as she realised what they were.

'I can't pay for these with company funds—these are your personal bills. Rates, electricity, phone?'

'Well pay them from your own money then and I'll pay you back once I get things sorted with Rebecca.'

'There's over a thousand dollars' worth of bills here! I don't have that kind of money!'

'Fine,' he said standing and snatching them back off her, 'when I really need your help, you're as good as useless—just get the fuck out of here.'

Shocked and hurt, she turned and walked quickly out of the office, closing the door behind her hard.

'Fucking hell!'

He threw the papers across the room and watched them scatter and see-saw through the air, each making its own way down to a different patch of carpet.

He would leave them there and see how long it took before Vivienne got off her fat arse and picked them up. No doubt she would be off at the local cafe crying into a cappuccino.

The chair creaked under his weight as he threw himself back into it. The coffee was too hot and he burnt his lip and swore again. If she wasn't such a good fuck he would have sacked her years ago.

Why were all the women in his life such useless bitches, he pondered.

He rang their doctor, her best friend and the local hospital. Nothing.

It wasn't like her to just disappear.

Now what?

He didn't have time for this shit.

Groaning, he got up and put his coat back on.

He walked down to the local police station and reported her missing.

'Have you eaten?' the old man asked her.

'No. Do I eat?' she asked earnestly, feeling a little silly.

'Yep. Nothing wrong with a faerie's appetite. Must be all the flying around. Sausages if you're lucky,' he said peering into the old fridge.

Over a dinner of sausage sandwiches they discussed the future.

'You can stay here for now. I've got a spare room. Bit dusty, but we can fix that up tomorrow,' he said, taking a mouthful of food.

She fell upon the food with abandon. He wondered how long it had been since she last ate.

'The police have already found the blood at the warehouse, the one where you woke up—the whole area was cordoned off this morning. Somebody, somewhere is going to realise you are missing at some point, and the police will probably will link your disappearance to that mess. You can't just hope they won't. You aren't the person you were.'

'You are going to need a new identity. You can't just turn up again and pretend you have been off on an adventure somewhere. Somebody tried to kill you *and they think they succeeded*—what would they do to you if you turned up alive again? Besides, unless you can learn to control your faerie talents you could put a whole lot of people in danger.' She nodded and continued eating.

'Before you can even think of walking around like a normal person I am going to have to teach you how to look human,' he said reaching for the tomato sauce. 'That will take a while. It's too late to start on that tonight. You need to really concentrate.'

Yes, concentrate—it has been a long time since he had to concentrate on anything himself. Was he going to be able to remember everything that he needed to teach her? He suddenly had the strange feeling that fate was at work. He would have to pull up his socks. She needed him. No one had needed him for a long time. He could not let her down.

He was secretly glad that her memory was failing her. She was on the edge of hysteria as it was. How she could have changed from a human being to a faerie was completely beyond him, but if he could keep her focused on learning how to use her new abilities, maybe she would have some direction, some purpose, for a while. Keep her going. Then she might not be quite so lost when it all came crashing down. He was not going to tell her anything about what he saw for now. She wasn't ready for it. Neither was he for that matter.

Once he'd finished eating, he showed her the room. It hadn't been used in a very long time; the carpet smelt dusty. He opened the window to let in some air and showed her where the sheets were kept, and then he toddled off to his own bed.

She was safe—she knew that—it was almost like an additional sense. The old man was genuine. She would have to ask him his name tomorrow. It hadn't even occurred to her tonight. Too much had been happening at once.

She made up the bed and lay down to sleep. She would have to clean the room tomorrow. The dust was stifling; she could feel it entering her lungs when she breathed. She stared at the darkness. She couldn't settle.

She got up and walked out to the kitchen to make a cup of tea. She waited for the kettle to boil and without even being aware of what she was doing she filled the sink with hot water and began scraping congealed food from the plates into the bin. She washed and dried and put away. She wiped the table and the sink and placed the empty wine bottles near the bin to take out in the morning. She glanced at her handiwork, and seeing nothing more to be done, she went back to bed—the tea completely forgotten. She had successfully distracted herself from thinking of anything at all, and was completely oblivious to the fact.

A New Day

Constable Ivan Peale and his partner Constable Leia Gardiner were doing an external inspection of the car when the café owner came over to talk to them. The car's owner had been reported missing.

'Is there something wrong with the car?' he asked, 'or with the lady who drove it here?'

'You know the owner?' asked Ivan opening his note book.

'No... but she was in the café two days ago. I think you'd better come over and have a word with Paul. He's one of my waiters—he told me some stuff this morning that I wish he'd told me yesterday—but he's new and young.' The proprietor was obviously worried.

Ivan turned to his partner, 'Can you finish up here and I'll go and have a chat?'

'No problem.'

The waiter was just a boy, earning some extra cash during the school holidays. He was nervous.

'Just tell him exactly what you told me,' the owner said to him placing a fatherly hand on his shoulder.

'Umm, the day before yesterday, she was here, the lady with that car,' he said pointing across the carpark. 'I thought it was my mate Todd at first, he has the same kinda car, but then she got out. She came in and I served her.'

'Is this the lady?' the constable asked showing him a picture.

'Yeah, but she was a lot fatter—I think she was pregnant.

The policeman nodded and made a note. 'Did she stay long?'

'Half an hour or so I think. It got really busy because it was lunch time and she just sat and had her coffee and talked on her mobile a bit. I was busy serving some other people and I looked up and a man had his

16

arm around her and was helping her out the door, she looked sick or something and I thought maybe she *was* pregnant and the baby was coming or something. And then I had to serve the coffees and later I noticed the car was still there, but if someone took her to the hospital it would be, wouldn't it?' The kid looked desperate; he was obviously kicking himself for not realising what was happening at the time.

'Possibly,' said the cop. He didn't want to give the poor kid any grief, for all they knew she was in some hospital safe and sound. 'What did the bloke look like?'

'He was a big guy, broad. Head shaved.'

'Bald or shaved fancy?'

'Bald.'

'Any facial hair or unusual facial features?'

'Nah—he was pretty ordinary. He looked like a plumber or something. He had those dark blue pants on and a dark shirt.'

'Any logos or anything else that stood out?'

'Nah.'

'Did you see which way they went?'

'Yeah, they turned into that street over there.'

'Okay, I'll get some details off you. We might need your help doing an identikit later.'

'Yeah, sure. Is the woman okay?'

'We don't know, but we haven't finished checking the hospitals yet and that's probably where she'll be.' The kid nodded, but he didn't look convinced.

Constable Gardiner joined him and they continued around the corner in the hope of finding a witness. There was a greengrocer whose shop opened out onto the street, wooden trolleys holding fruit and vegetables. He seemed to be an obvious starting point. They hit the jackpot first-time.

'Yes, I saw them. I was filling up the fruit bins out here. She didn't look very well, he was helping her along. I asked him if he wanted me to call an ambulance. The man told me she was just a bit under the weather and said thank you anyway, so I went back to my stacking.'

'Did you see where they went?' asked Constable Gardiner.

'There was a red car, parked just down the road, a Toyota. An old Corolla. They drove off down that way,' he said pointing west.

'I don't suppose you remember the number plate?' said Peale.

'Not all of it, but the first three letters were "S -Y - D" couldn't forget that, could I?'

'How would you describe the man?' Gardiner asked.

'He was bald and he had workman's clothes on, dark blue. He had his sleeves rolled up and there were tatts on his arms. He wasn't very tall, but he was solid.'

Back at the station, a cross-check of the stolen car database revealed that the car had been stolen sometime after 7:30 AM on the day she went missing. It had not been recovered yet. Ivan updated the job, indicating that the car may have been used in an abduction, and flagged it as priority one.

She woke to the smell of bacon. She pulled on the dressing gown and went out in to the kitchen.

He looked up from the frying pan. 'There's a spare towel in the bathroom if you want a bath. Matches for the water heater are on the sill.'

She stumbled bleary eyed into the bathroom. An old-fashioned gas water heater was attached to the wall over one end of the tub. She hadn't seen one since her grandmother's place in Leichhardt. It had been a bastard to light. This one was too. She remembered her mother telling off her sister Prue for splashing too much—afraid they would douse the pilot light and flood the place with gas.

She wondered where Prue was now. It had been years since they last spoke; it had not been pleasant. Suddenly she realised that she had just remembered something. She has been a normal little girl, with a mother and a father and a sister. The more she tried to stretch her memory the more it faded away. She could still not remember her own name. She tried very hard to be patient, to relax, she thought about the feel of the warm water on her skin, but she was too restless. The bath was heavenly, but she didn't linger; the smell of bacon from the kitchen was overwhelming. She dried off as best she could, leaving her wings to drip and squashing them into the gown. She was going to have to get some clothes somehow.

When she came out he was sitting at the kitchen table and gestured to the plate laid opposite. It was piled high with bacon, eggs and fried mushrooms.

'I never asked you last night—what's your name?' she asked before taking a mouthful of bacon.

'Andrew. Andrew Roswald. But call me Andy.'

She swallowed her bacon, 'Andy. I'm sorry, but I still can't remember my own name. I did just remember that I have a sister called

Prue though, so maybe you are right, it will all come back eventually,' she said and sighed.

They ate in silence for a while, and then Andy laid down his fork, 'Time for you to think up a new name, and we'll have to work on a new face as well. You might need it if you have to disappear.'

'A new face?' she said incredulously, 'Get plastic surgery you mean?'

'No—you can do it yourself—you just need to learn how. You can look however you want. How about I call you Renee for the time being. If anyone asks you're my daughter,' he paused and looked at her.

'When I first saw you up in the rafters of the workshop—when I realised that you were lost and that you weren't one of the nasty faeries—I thought you might have been …'

'… Ah, it doesn't matter now.'

He stacked the dishes by the sink. 'Thanks for this—' he said gruffly and gestured to the kitchen, 'I have been letting things go for too long. Gotta stop dwelling on the past.'

He motioned for her to follow him.

'Can't have you running around in that thing,' he said gesturing at her dressing gown, 'what'll the neighbours say?'

He shuffled into his bedroom and opened the wardrobe. One half was suspended in time. Neatly hanging were racks of women's skirts, blouses, slacks and dresses. Although the clothes were old, they were classic styles and would not look out of place. There were printed silky blouses, elegant flowing trousers and tight-waisted dresses with halter necks. Most of the blouses were halter necks too. He caught her expression, 'she used to wear a jacket over the top,' he explained. 'No back—much easier for flying—and she could carry the jacket.'

It made sense.

'She looked after herself; she could get away with it, even at a hundred and forty.'

She stared at him. She must have heard wrong.

'Yep; not immortal, just live a lot longer. I don't know how long though, she died young for a faerie, a lot of them live past 300. God only knows with you, maybe you're starting from zero, or maybe you don't end at all.'

She was not comfortable with this line of conversation. She wanted to be normal.

He left her to try on the clothes while he went out and did the dishes.

The clothes were a good fit.

How could she ever repay him? Not just for his time and the food and shelter, but for his kindness? He had so little; but she had nothing to give him in return. She had no money, and no possessions. She would help around the house as much as possible for now until she could think up a better way to repay him.

Andy was conscious of the fact that she was running on automatic; survival mode had kicked in. For the time being he needed to drum as much knowledge into her as possible so she could keep herself safe. One slip up and she would be in deep trouble. Sooner or later she would crack, and he needed to make sure that everything he taught her was second nature by that point. Until then he would try and keep her mind occupied.

Later that day he taught her the command to dim her faerie glow. She could almost pass as human without it—if she could hide her wings and her eyes. Her eyes were like opals. The irises were flecked with different colours, mostly greens, but layered like an opal so that they changed depending on the angle of the light. Sunglasses would hide them in a pinch, but the wings were just too big to hide. He tried to teach her the command to make her wings disappear, it was similar to the others—a word and a mental image—but she could not get it right. By lunch time she was frustrated and angry. He called it off.

'We'll try that spell again tomorrow. Maybe it's because you haven't mastered your wings yet. Do you know how to move them?'

'No,' she admitted.

'Right, well, once we have had some food, we'll go somewhere where we can practice. Once you've sorted that out you might be able to do the other.'

The building they were heading to was on the opposite side of the industrial area. It was well away from where she had met her demise. There was still too much police action over that side, and he did not want to be seen by any passing coppers. She was much less conspicuous hiding in his pocket now that she could dim her glow. Nobody gave him a second glance.

They had to cross an old, overgrown park, tucked between dilapidated workers' cottages. In the centre was an ancient Moreton Bay Fig tree. Its thick dark canopy shaded the ground around it, its ancient arms stretched out from the centre in all directions, dipping back towards the ground and melting into it in large gnarly suckers. It was huge and dark and…

Renee held her breath. She knew this tree. She hated this tree…

…she was young, maybe eight? Sunday best dress on. They had stopped at a park on the way home from visiting Grandma. Prue was snarling at her, trying to snatch the necklace from her neck. Prue was always trying to get it off her. Mum never paid any attention; if dad had been there…

She had run from her, dodging her groping hands, desperate to avoid them in case she broke the chain of her most treasured possession once and for all. The Fig tree was huge; if she could climb up into the gap in the branches she would be safe. Prue would never follow; she would be too scared of ripping her lovely dress.

The tree was dark and twisted. She had climbed quickly, barely touching the tree as she hurtled up from branch to branch. Prue had called her a rude name and then gone to tell tales to mum. Her dress was still in one piece, so she probably wouldn't be in too much trouble.

Her hand felt funny. She looked at it. The tree felt sticky. She tried to lift her hand, but it wouldn't come. She pulled harder.

Then she heard the laugh; low, evil, mocking laughter. It was the tree.

'You can't hide from me, little one,' it purred.

Her head felt odd. The lights were fading. She felt like she was melting into the tree.

She wrenched her hand free, and fell down, down, down…

…she took a deep breath.

Andy noticed her discomfort.

'Don't worry; we aren't going anywhere near old Kraken'.

She was surprised. 'Can you feel it too?' she asked.

'Yes. Nancy gave me the ability. She didn't like him at all.'

'You talk as if it is a sentient being.'

'It is.'

She looked at the tree again. Tucked amongst its branches were chains and pendants.

'What are those things?' she asked.

'Amulets. Some of the local teenagers like to scare each other; play at witch craft. Satanism. I think the tree actually absorbs some of their fear. Feeds on it.'

'I've been here before,' she said.

His brow creased.

'When I was a little girl, I didn't like this tree at all.'

'This is an old faerie tree; a doorway. But it is an evil one. So don't go near it.'

She watched it until it was lost from sight. She had a strange feeling, an intense feeling, that she should not turn her back on it.

They crossed the park and entered the industrial area. There was an old shed, clad with timber that looked like an old barn. He expertly picked the padlock on the side door and they slipped inside. One half was full of stacked wooden crates, but there was a vacant area big enough for their purposes. Once he had made sure that the barn had no cameras he took her out of his pocket and she returned to full size.

'I said before, I don't think I can teach you anything about flying. I imagine you need to feel all those muscles and joints for yourself. But maybe…' he stood and thought for a moment.

'Can you feel them now? Can you work out which muscles make them move?' he asked her. She shrugged her shoulders. Then she pushed her shoulders back. She tightened the muscles of her buttocks and stretched her spine. Nothing. She couldn't feel anything different.

'Nothing,' she said despondently.

'OK. It is a long shot, but it's worth a try. I'm going to push against your wings. He stood behind her and pushed her wings together between his palms. 'Can you feel that?' he asked.

'Yes! Yes! I can.'

'OK—gently now—see if you can push back.' She stretched the strange new muscles and he eased the pressure. 'See if you can do in reverse.' This was harder. She moved them inward a little, but then ended up pushing them out again. He moved his hands between her wings and gently pushed outward this time. She could feel another set of new muscles come into play and contracted them. A couple more practice runs and she could move her wings open and closed by herself. Fifteen minutes of practice and she could flutter them at will, even pausing in mid-stroke. He got her to shrink herself again and redo the wing exercises, then for the next hour they ran through a series of commands one after another in quick succession until she could perform each of the things he had taught her without hesitation.

'Excellent—you need a good bit of practice before we start on flying—need to strengthen those muscles—but you're gettin' it all right,' he positively beamed. 'Time to head home. What shall we have for dinner? I think this calls for a celebration.'

'How can I repay you? I don't have any money. You can't keep feeding me—it's just not right,' she said guiltily.

'Right, schmight. Don't get yer knickers in a twist. We weren't rich, but my Nancy made sure I'd be OK before she passed on. We'll manage.' When she was about to protest he added, 'If you feel you have to repay me, you can later—and we can give the local drug dealing scum a kick up the butt in the process. But that's later—first you gotta learn all this other stuff.'

He looked around the barn to make sure they had not left anything amiss.

'Ready?' he asked. She nodded and returned to fairy size. He picked her up and slipped her into his pocket. They headed home. None of this seemed real to her. She was going through the motions, always expecting to wake up and find it was a dream. The exercises kept her from going crazy, so she concentrated on practising the movements and remembering everything he taught her.

But she had to admit; she couldn't wait to start flying.

Philip

Constable Gardiner had impounded Rebecca's car and had obtained a warrant to search her apartment, but it had turned up nothing unusual. It was quite an expensive apartment; the rent would have been high.

Rebecca Cole's phone and credit cards had not been used since her disappearance and her handbag had not been found. All of the checks with the local hospitals had come back negative. No new mothers had come in matching her description; no pregnant women in distress, no cadavers. A media release was being prepared and would be aired on TV appealing for help from the public. There had been no new leads.

Until now…

The stolen Corolla had been found; burnt out and dumped at the docks. The number plates had been removed, but there was enough paintwork left for Constable Peale to determine it had been a red car and the compliance plates were still readable.

The fire hadn't completely done its job. Caught in the remains of the back-seat, forensics found a vicious looking knife; they didn't think they'd be able to get anything off it. Gardiner and Peale had taken a hairbrush from Mrs Cole's flat for a DNA comparison, just in case.

The car was not far from the warehouse they had been called to earlier in the week. It was possible that the two events were linked. They reported the find to Detective Inspector Hayes in homicide. DI Hayes decided it was time to find out more about the husband and sent the two constables off to find Mr Philip Cole.

The two constables tracked Philip Cole down to his office in the city. Gardiner was a little surprised that he was at work, considering that his pregnant wife was missing—but then again, they were separated.

Philip was in his office with a client when they arrived, so they took a seat in the reception area to wait. Five minutes later, the door to his office opened and he escorted his client into the reception area. His secretary went over to him and whispered. He turned and looked directly at Gardiner, it was a lingering look, meeting her eyes and then sliding down over her entire body. He glanced briefly at Peale and then turned his back on them and spoke quietly to his secretary. Constable Peale discretely raised his eyebrows at Gardiner and she rolled her eyes in response. The secretary finished her conversation with Philip and nodded, making her way over to Gardiner.

'He can see you both now, if you'd like to go in.'

'Thanks.'

They entered his office and Peale closed the door behind them.

'I'm Constable Leia Gardiner and this is Constable Ivan Peale,' she was already pissed off, she was not going to let this man intimidate her. 'Sorry to bother you at work, sir,' she said in her most formal police voice, 'but we've received a few tip offs regarding your wife's disappearance.'

'Not a problem at all,' he said waving her towards a chair, 'please, take a seat. How can I help?' The leering was bad, but there was something else too. Something about him made her skin crawl. She ignored the offer of a seat. A lot of people got nervous when they had to talk to the police and acted in an unnatural fashion. They subconsciously tried to project an image of strength, or helpfulness, or subservience. But this was different; there was something she couldn't put her finger on…

'Well to start with, we'd like to get your permission to analyse a DNA sample from your wife. We have a hairbrush from her flat that we'd like to send for forensics,' said Constable Gardiner.

'Do you think you've found her?' Philip said, his face turning a shade paler.

'No Sir, this is just so that we have a sample for comparison should anything turn up. Could you sign this form please?'

He signed it and passed it back to her. His bravado had slipped a notch, she couldn't help feeling pleased.

'We have found your wife's car, and we have a witness that saw your wife leave the cafe with a large bald man wearing workman's clothes. Do you know anyone that might match that description?' Constable Peal asked him.

Constable Gardiner thought she saw a flicker of panic in Philip's face, but he recovered quickly.

'No. I don't know any bald men.'

'I understand that you are separated from your wife?' said Constable Peale.

'Yes, for a couple of months now.'

'Was it an amicable split?'

'Oh yes! We both just needed some space. Rebecca has some very definite ideas about the baby and how we are going to raise it and I just don't think I'm ready for all that. We are trying to work out how we are going to juggle everything.'

'So the baby wasn't planned then?' asked Constable Gardiner.

'No. It was a bit of a surprise. We had agreed that we weren't going to have children, but when she got pregnant she changed her mind. I still don't know if I want to be a parent, but no doubt that will change once I see the baby. A lot of people have told me that's what happens. We aren't making any big decisions until the baby's born. She decided to move out because she thought all my negativity might be bad for the baby. Wanted positive karma or something.'

'Is she employed at the moment?' asked Constable Peale.

'Yes. She's a pay clerk at Berry's Transport. But she went on Maternity leave a couple of weeks ago.'

'So when was the last time you saw Rebecca?' asked Gardiner.

About a week ago. I was supposed to meet her for brunch the day she went missing, but I was held up in a meeting and was late. She was already gone when I got there.'

Gardiner made a note to go back to the café owner and check if Mr Cole had actually turned up.

'So you have no idea who the bald man could be?'

'No. I don't know anyone like that.'

'A witness has told us that he saw her drive off with this man. The car they left in was stolen earlier in the day…'

'Stolen! Has she been kidnapped?'

'It's too early to know, but it is possible. We will be making an appeal for information to the general public via the media, sir. If anyone should contact you directly, we need to know straight away.'

Philip nodded in a daze. Gardiner couldn't make him out.

'There is one other thing…' Peale added, 'the media release will say that we have grave concerns for her safety. We don't want to be pessimistic, but the circumstances are suspicious. There isn't much else we can tell you at this stage.'

He is bewildered, thought Gardiner. Not distraught, not horror struck or grieved—he is bewildered.

'There is one more thing we need to know, Sir...' Gardiner added, 'we have the report you made to the duty officer regarding Rebecca's disappearance, with the details of your movements on that day. We just need to confirm where you went on the day Rebecca disappeared; when she didn't show for lunch.'

'Oh! Didn't I mention that?' he said pulling himself back together (with almost alarming speed Gardiner thought).

'There is no record,' said Gardiner re-opening her notebook.

'Well, I tried to call her again before I left the café, but there was no answer. So I sent her a text. Then I went back to the office and got my secretary to grab a sandwich for me before my next client arrived. Then I was busy in the office with meetings—at some point I tried to call her again—but no luck. So I dropped by her flat on my way home, must've been about 6:30, but still no answer on her phone or at the door and her car wasn't in her usual spot, so I went home.

'By the time I got home and had dinner it was a bit late to call again—so I thought I'd leave it until morning. Then I tried again, and her doctor, and the hospital, and her friends. And then I went to the Police Station.

'It's been days. Tell me, honestly, what are the chances she is still alive. I don't want to think about her being dead, but I can't stop myself. This is so unlike her; especially in her condition.'

'I'm sorry sir, but I really can't say, there isn't enough to go on yet. The circumstances are very suspicious. We will let you know as soon as we have more information.' Peale said.

'I see. Thank you,' he said rather abruptly.

'Would you like us to drive you home, sir? You could probably do with some rest,' asked Peale.

'No. No, I'm fine. Better to keep busy.'

'We'll show ourselves out,' said Gardiner, keen to be away from him.

He nodded brusquely. Peale had a quick word with his secretary and they left the building.

'What did you say to the secretary?' Gardiner asked.

'Just told her to keep an eye on him, I think he is a bit stunned. To be honest, I'm not quite sure what to make of him. Very open and honest about their relationship wasn't he. Not hiding the fact that he didn't want the kid. Either he is extremely naïve, extremely stupid. Or he seriously thinks she is going to turn up fit as a flea,' said Peale.

'Or he's already thought it out, and knows that someone is going to blab about the reason they separated and it was better that we hear it from him first,' said Gardiner.

'True. But if he has premeditated her abduction and murder, what would he gain from it? Okay, so he wouldn't have to pay child support—but that isn't much of a gain—compared to the risk of being charged with murder. She wasn't rich was she?' he asked.

'I haven't checked her finances yet, but that is number one on my list when we get back.'

Gardiner was sitting in a chair opposite DI Hayes and Peale was balanced on the edge of the desk. They had just finished briefing Detective Inspector Hayes on their interview with Mr Cole. Hayes had his feet on the desk and a forensic report balanced on his legs.

'Sounds to me like Mr Cole is not telling us everything.'

'There is something that just doesn't gel,' said Gardiner.

'And he's a complete sleaze,' said Peale, 'You should have seen the way he looked at Gardiner, no shame at all!'

'Please, don't remind me, I'm about to eat lunch,' she said pulling a face.

'Bit of a Neanderthal is he? Do you want out, or are you okay?'

'I'm fine boss, that little jerk isn't going to put me off the job.'

'Excellent. I think we will keep an eye on Mr Cole, but in the meantime, can you get that hairbrush down to George, please.'

Gardiner picked up the snap lock bag containing the brush and left the room.

Hayes was flicking back and forth through the pages of the forensic report. A living, loving human being reduced to a hairbrush in a clinical plastic bag, he mused. The report was the analysis of the blood and tissue found in the warehouse.

He wondered what Rebecca Cole's blood type was. They should be able to get that from her medical records.

'Ivan, do you want to give Mr Cole a ring and find out the name of Mrs Cole's doctor? Get him to write up an authority to give us access to Mrs Cole's medical records too. Then if you've got time—' said Hayes.

'I'll pay the doctor a visit. I'm onto it. You think the two cases are related?' Ivan asked, glancing at the warehouse report.

'Could be. It's worth a look. Make sure you find out what Rebecca's blood type was.'

Ivan got up to go and make the calls.

Some tissue (possibly human) had been found at the warehouse. The report contained a DNA analysis of it. The next paragraph made him pause. The tissue samples were believed to be placental. They would have the results back on the hairbrush in a few days. He would be interested in seeing the two DNA results side-by-side.

Faerie Rings

Once Renee had the hang of which muscles to use, she mastered flying quickly. They visited the barn daily, practising flying for hours at a time. She was flying around with ease now, and could even change size mid-flight. It was exhilarating; a childhood dream come true. It was almost enough to make up for all the horrors of the past few days; she had to keep mentally shaking herself to make sure she wasn't dreaming.

Andy was very pleased with her progress, and they were going to have another go at hiding her wings.

'Now, do you remember...' he stopped suddenly in mid-sentence and began to scan the rafters.

'What is it?' she whispered, sensing something was wrong.

'Trouble. I can't see them, but I can feel them. They're up there somewhere. Time to go.' She shrank and flew quickly into his pocket and he made his way out of the barn and around the corner.

'Damn them!' he exclaimed angrily. 'Fifty years and they still won't leave me alone.'

'What was it?' she asked. She had felt something, but wasn't sure if it was real or if she had just picked up on his anxiety.

'Once we're away from them,' he said and disappeared into an old service lane.

From there he slipped over a low wall into an underground car park. He crouched low and wound his way between the cars towards the lift. There was a young man already waiting for the lift and as soon as the bell rang Andy walked quickly over to it and joined him. The lift emptied into a foyer and then they were out onto a bustling street. He took a seat at an outdoor cafe, and picked up the paper. He ordered a coffee when the waiter appeared. She could tell he was searching. Not with his eyes—with his mind.

'Can't feel them anymore. I think we've given them the slip.'

The waiter appeared with his coffee and he stirred sugar into it, still probing with his mind. She could feel the energy of it, even if she didn't know how he did it.

'Can't talk here. People will think I'm nuts,' he whispered hiding his face behind the newspaper. 'I'll finish this coffee and then we'll slip home.'

She peeped out of the top of his pocket. Two police officers were sauntering towards the cafe.

'Cops at the counter,' she whispered.

'I see 'em. Can't leave too quickly—will draw attention.' They were talking to the young man at the counter. 'You keep an eye on them for me—let me know if they get too interested.'

The old man finished his coffee, placed some coins on the table, neatly folded the newspaper and walked away.

'No. They didn't look twice.'

'Excellent.'

Once they were home he put the kettle on and started making ham sandwiches for lunch. He shook his head; he was annoyed.

'You need to know this,' he said, 'it's important,' he said placing the sandwiches on the table.

'When Nancy and I came to this country we hadn't been here five minutes when we ran into that lot. They can sense you and they sensed Nancy. They're faeries same as you—but you don't want anything to do with them—they are bad news. Their queen is a monster.

'See this ring on my finger?' he asked her. She looked over the sandwich she was eating at his finger. The ring was gold, filigree, and made in a Celtic design.

'This is the pretty gift that can take away your freedom. Don't ever accept a ring like this unless you saw it made and heard the spells that were bound to it *and know what they mean*. Otherwise you are done for. This one Nancy made for me, and I saw it made and I was happy to take it. It gives me some of the faerie magicks. It lets me feel when those bastards are near. I could communicate with Nancy too—even if we were miles apart. And she made it so I could take it off and put it on again anytime I wanted to. And that's the important bit; you have to add that otherwise if you take it off it disappears.'

After they had finished eating, he had an idea.

'Here, touch my forehead right here.' She reached up and placed her hand on the side of his head.

'Another thing the ring can do is show you my memories—if I let you.'

She felt a strange vibration run up her arm and suddenly it felt like she was inside a small darkened space, like she was inside her own head with her eyes shut. The images when they came, weren't like a movie or a photo; some parts were hazy—greyed and out of focus—like these parts weren't important. Other parts were crystalline in their colour and detail, sharp and brilliant. She could hear and smell in these memories too.

She was seeing through Andy's eyes. A woman was standing next to him; she looked worried, and a little scared. She could feel Andy take the woman's hand in his own, although she didn't see him do it. She could sense that this woman was Nancy without actually knowing how she knew it. Her senses were extended beyond the normal five.

It was night time; there was a heavy layer of snow on the ground. It was dark but there were lights in the distance. Flickering lights. Noise. A crowd of people getting closer, screams and shouts. Anger. They were coming for Andy and Nancy. An old woman came out of one of the houses nearby.

'What are you still doing here?' she chastised them. 'They aren't pretending! They are inbred, demented fools. Nothing I say will change their minds—you have to run now or they will kill you!'

Andy and Nancy stepped towards an ancient oak tree. Nancy shrank them both, wrapped her arms around him and flew with him high into the branches. They entered a knot-hole in the tree and stood within a hollow in the heart of the tree.

'You have to keep moving, you can't stay here.' The old oak tree told them. Looking out of the tree through the knot-hole they saw the mob arrive.

'That way,' the tree told them, and a wooden archway appeared on the far side of the hollow and shimmered before them. 'You'll be safe there. You can depend on Old Blue.'

Nancy placed her hands on the tree's wooden walls and gave him a surge of faerie energy. The tree sighed, contented.

They passed through the archway and magically entered another tree in another place. Old Blue.

The door sealed behind them.

'What just happened?' Nancy asked the new tree, alarmed.

'Oaken has sealed the doorway on his side, he is afraid.'

Suddenly the door frame began to smoke and char. Old Blue howled in pain and sealed the doorway from his side. The link was severed and the burning stopped.

'They've burnt him, haven't they?'

'Yes.' Old Blue sobbed.

Nancy was crying, as she put a comforting hand on the tree.

The image blurred to darkness and then a new image appeared.

Nancy and Andy were standing at the base of a towering gum tree. It was daytime. They looked at each other and then started to move forward through a forest of flowering eucalypts. It was a hot day and the smell of evaporating eucalyptus oil was strong. Brittle leaves crunched under their feet, and the sound of a kookaburra startled them to a halt. It was a strange new world that they had entered. One minute they had been in thick snow, fleeing from something (his mind refused to dwell on that) and the next, they had stepped from a tree into blinding sunshine and oppressive heat.

Andy's voice broke over the vision—

'This was when we left Scotland forever. We didn't know it at the time, but we came out deep in the Blue Mountains; west of here. Oaken and Old Blue helped save us.'

The pair in the vision continued on.

'Can you feel it?' Nancy asked.

'Yes,' he replied

They walked for miles, searching for the source of the attraction. They were about to approach a river when they heard voices, and quickly moved behind the cover of some trees to watch.

On the other side of the river a young woman emerged from the trees; crying. She walked to the river and sat down, curled up tight, her head on her raised knees and her arms wrapping herself into a bundle of misery. A few moments later a young man approached her and put an arm around her shoulders.

'Are you okay? What happened?'

She turned a tear-stained face to him.

'She said no. She won't let us marry. You have to go—you have to run! If you stay she will enslave you like the others. *She took my wings away.*' She sobbed into her knees.

He stared at her.

'Can't you make them re-appear?'

'No. She took all my powers away. She said she will give them back to me when I can show that I am a loyal member of the swarm. When I can behave.' The girl broke into anguished sobs again.

'Come with me. Run away with me!'

'I can't. I can't cross the river. If I do, I will die. She's bound me to our land. You have to go. She is going to come after you, to enslave you or kill you—to teach me a lesson about getting involved with humans. You have to leave now. The ring I gave you will still protect you as long as you leave this place—she won't be able to sense your presence. If she can't see you, she can't find you. Go!'

He twisted the ring around and around his finger.

'Somehow, I will find a way to rescue you.'

He held her close, a last lingering kiss, and then he stood up and waded across the river. A final wave from the other side and then he disappeared into the trees.

She returned to her heartbroken sobbing.

A minute later a tall faerie woman appeared, striding out of the bushes. She looked grim; her wings were blood red with black veins.

'What have you done?' the woman said in a low ominous voice.

'You'll never find him now—he's gone. Before you took my powers I hid him from you!'

'You have pure faerie blood. I will not have the life force of our clan diluted by any more human blood. If you cross me, you will pay the penalty. Reveal him or die.'

'I would rather die.'

'So be it.'

A sword materialised in the woman's hand. One slash and the girl lay sprawled and lifeless on the riverbank, blood draining from her body.

The murderer pushed her body into the water with the tip of her foot, disgust on her face. She watched as the body dissolved into sparkling atoms, each little spark emerging from the water with a tiny eruption and drifting off with the breeze. The pool of blood on the bank was the only evidence of the crime.

Andy and Nancy stood unable to move.

The witch faerie looked up suddenly. They knew at the same moment that she could sense their presence.

In an instant, Nancy had shrunk Andy to the size of a beetle and held him in her hand, and then she shrank as well and fled. She was flying through the undergrowth, evading the pursuing menace, heading back to Old Blue.

Andy could feel the power emanating from Old Blue as Nancy flew straight for him. In a flash they were inside the enormous faerie tree, and the tree, sensing they were in danger again, closed the door behind them. It was like the door was made of glass, because they could still see the trees outside. Strangely, the witch faerie passed by the tree without a second glance.

'Can't she see you?' Nancy asked the tree.

'No. She is not a tree spirit. The trees are silent to her, and our doorways are hidden.'

The memory ended and Renee felt herself falling back out of her own head and into the light of the current day.

She blinked. 'Do you know what happened to the boy?'

'No. But he probably would have known straight away that she was dead—because of the ring. When she died, the faerie ring she gave him probably would have unravelled and turned back into hair. Mine didn't when Nancy died because Nancy was powerful enough to put a special spell on it. She had good reason to believe that I would still need it if she died. These faeries are weak. They don't know a lot of the old magicks; the queen likes to keep them that way.'

'That fairy, with the red and black wings—she was the queen?'

'Yes. We ran into her again later. As far as I know she is still alive and still controls the others.'

'Why do they put up with her? Why don't they rebel against her?'

'They did; the Great Faerie War. It was a disaster. The slaughter was incredible. Those that are left have given up all hope of beating her.'

They sat a while lost in their own thoughts. It seemed strange to Renee that a gift as wonderful as this could be coupled with such terrible evil. How could anyone in control of such wondrous powers want to harm someone else?

'Can any fairy make a ring?' she asked him.

'Yep.' He said shaking himself out of his reverie, 'and now I want you to make one for me. But it has to have all these things—' he said dragging the pen and paper towards him.

'First and foremost, it can be removed without dissolving, second, we can use it to communicate with each other, thirdly I can detect when you are near, as opposed to those other monsters. That should be all it needs,' he said putting the pen back down.

'This sort of magick is intense. We need to make sure we are safe first because it will take a lot out of you.'

'Will it hurt?'

'No,' he said. He got up and bolted the front door, then disappeared to check the others.

'You'd better go and lie on your bed,' he said as he returned. He dragged the kitchen chair into her bedroom and sat down next to her.

'Okay, pluck a hair from your head and hold it in your right hand by one end. Now using your left thumb and forefinger, slide them from the top of the hair to the bottom. Yep, that's right. Now—here are the words—say them out loud as you wind it around this finger,' he said holding out his hand.

'Eev-rakh, Loww-ir, Rye,' she said, winding the hair around his finger. Suddenly she felt an incredible pulling sensation travelling from her heart and along her arms. It felt like it was pulling something out of her body. Several other strange words followed and when she had finished she collapsed back on the bed. She felt like her body was made of metal, pulling her down into the mattress. He held up his hand and she could see a beautiful filigree ring, similar to the one he already wore, but with a slightly different pattern. It twinkled and sparkled for a moment then settled back to a normal sheen.

'Well done!' he said. 'First try. You're a natural. Get some sleep. We'll test it later.'

She didn't need to be told, she was already drifting off.

It is completely dark. Then out of the darkness, two long, thin golden snakes appeared. They writhed around each other, twisting into incredibly intricate patterns; forming a living, moving ring. Their eyes flashed a fiery red; their skins were patterned and textured gold.

Slowly the two snakes unwound themselves and stretched out in opposite directions straining to reach two figures half hidden in the darkness. She could see no features, only their glowing opalescent eyes. She felt an intense loneliness, and she knew that she would never be with her own kind—human or fairy—because she was both, and she was neither.

Detective Inspector Tom Hayes doubted very much that Rebecca Cole would be found alive.

He was naturally suspicious of the husband; more women were killed by their partners or ex-partners than by anyone else. He was probably more suspicious of Philip than the two uniforms were, but he wasn't going to influence them, he wanted a nice clean investigation. He hadn't met Philip Cole yet, so it was a bit early for him to form an opinion either way. But then, he had seen cold-blooded killers lie without skipping a beat.

Whether Philip had anything to do with the disappearance of his wife was yet to be seen, but he wasn't going to discount him this early in the game. Men had murdered their wives in jealousy plenty of times before, especially if a baby turned out to be someone else's. He needed some more background on both of them.

It was just after 10 PM when she awoke. The dream had disturbed her and left her with a deep sense of melancholy.

The house was dark. She wondered if the old man was asleep, and instantly she knew he was. His ring told her so—it was like a thought flying into her mind from nowhere. She could fly now, and she could make herself small, and she could dim her glow. But she still didn't know who she was.

Why couldn't she remember?!

The more she thought about it the more frustrated and angry she became.

She needed something to trigger her memory…

The warehouse—where she woke up—it was the first thing she could remember.

Maybe if she went back there?

She shot off into the night.

There were no police around and she slipped easily through a gap in the corrugated iron. There were chalk lines. The smell was terrible. Hovering metres above the mess, she could see her own silhouette pressed into the blood. It was ghastly; a death mural.

Looking closer, she could see her tiny footprints leaving the blood.

A sudden surge of anger flushed inside her. She screamed at the bloody stain in fury and despair. How could someone have done this? They had tried to kill her!

She landed on the floor, staggering. Why did they want to kill her? Why? Why live through this travesty to be alone like this? She knew in her heart that she had never done anything to hurt anyone. None of this was fair.

She sat huddled in a corner sobbing; a tiny lost creature.
Andy was all she had now.

He was tired and he should be home. Tom rubbed his eyes and read through the report again. The blood at the warehouse was the same blood type as Rebecca. The DNA results from the blood had not come back yet, but the DNA from the tissue sample was a match.

Rebecca Cole was no more. Whatever had happened to her, there was no way she could have lost that much blood and lived. The next question was 'why?' Then they might be able to answer the 'who?' He had arranged for the police divers to do an inspection of the harbour near the docks first thing in the morning. It seemed the most likely place to find something; it wasn't far from the warehouse or the burnt-out car. He would stop by there first in the morning. Then he would have to visit the husband and give him the bad news.

Bill

When Andy awoke, he knew immediately that she wasn't in the house.

Damn!

Where would she be?

Hopefully she was just out practising her new skills somewhere. He hoped to God that she hadn't started remembering the past. She wasn't strong enough yet to be running around looking for people that she knew in her old life. He just hoped that she had the sense to stay concealed—to just watch them for now. They hadn't even invented an alibi for her yet.

It was too soon!

He got up and made himself some breakfast, but he wasn't really hungry. He picked at it while he stared at the clock.

Finally he got up and went for a walk.

Maybe Bruce had seen her light flitting about.

The day was fine and the water was clear; good for the search at the docks. Nothing of interest had been found so far, but they still had another couple of areas to check out.

Something was nagging at him. DI Tom Hayes walked the couple of blocks to the warehouse. He climbed past the police tape and slipped the key into the padlock. Apart from some chalk marks, the scene was as it had been found.

The culprits hadn't cared less about the mess they made near the scene of the crime—there were at least two sets of shoe prints traipsing in and out of blood—but they had managed to move the body out of the warehouse without leaving a trail at all. There were no drips, splatters, drag marks or prints heading towards any of the doors. They must have bagged the body before they left the building. Half sloppy, half professional; odd.

The pool of blood had the ghostly shape of a prone figure moulded into it. The body had laid there long enough for the blood to start to set around it, and then somehow the body had been lifted clear, leaving the pattern intact. They had not even left any marks where they had slid their hands under the body to lift it. Apart from a tiny trail of indentations and bloody prints left by an insect, there were no imperfections in the body imprint at all. A crane perhaps? He looked up. Nope, the warehouse didn't have one. But why go to such trouble when you've already made a dog's breakfast of it all?

Maybe they were interrupted before they could do the final clean up?

A tiny green sparkle flitted across the wall and disappeared, distracting him for a moment.

'God, these Christmas beetles are everywhere his year.'

When he got back to the office he had the missing persons case transferred over to homicide.

The policeman's arrival had startled Renee, and made her realise she had to be more careful—she had to get her shit together. She flew home.

She was partway there when she sensed that Andy wasn't home. His ring was like a beacon calling to her from the barn. He was looking for her, no doubt. She changed direction.

When she got there, she found him sitting on a crate. He sensed her as she got nearer and stood up.

'Wondered where you'd got to,' he said, looking at her curiously as she returned to full size. 'Have you remembered something?'

'No. I went to the warehouse—the one where I woke up. I needed to see it. I was hoping it might trigger something,' she said sadly, 'I wish I hadn't.'

'Still a mess is it?'

'Yes.'

'I think you could probably do with an outing. Take your mind off things for a bit. Do you some good.'

'Yeah, maybe you're right,' she said despondently. She didn't really want to do anything, but if she did nothing she would end up thinking, and she didn't want that either.

'I want you to come on a little excursion with me. But before we do that, I've got something else to teach you. We need to be able to communicate without speaking—telepathy—faeries call it shil labhair. I don't want to be talking aloud while you're hiding in my pocket. I may be daft but I don't want to look it.'

He took a few steps away from her and held up his hand.

'Concentrate on this ring,' he said. 'Now think about saying something to me—anything you like—but don't say it out loud. Just imagine the words in your head.'

As soon as she began to picture the ring in her mind she saw a glowing strand of hair unwind from the mental image in her head and spiral towards the ring on the old man's finger. It wrapped around the ring; a glowing cord linking the two of them together.

'Can you hear me?' she thought, *'I can see the link. Can anyone else see it or is it just in my head?'* As she thought, the cord oscillated—the wave sliding along the cord towards Andy. Another began to travel back towards her and a fraction of a second later, his voice appeared in her thoughts.

'It's just in your mind. As soon as you think of breaking the thread, it will break,' he thought to her.

Without really wanting to she thought of the thread breaking and the image slipped away.

'Oh! I didn't mean to do that,' she said aloud.

'Yes—it's very easy to break, especially if there are a bunch of rogue faeries flying around your ears screeching. You'll need to learn to block them out.'

'Why would they do that?'

'Because they like to meddle and because it is considered bad manners to hold a silent conversation in front of another faerie. But that's their rules—not ours. They have no trouble intruding where they aren't wanted, so we don't play by their rules.

'Now, try again, but this time once we've got the connection I want you to go for a walk. You need to be able to keep the thread going, while other stuff is distracting you. Can't be tripping over your own feet while you're thought-talking. Head off down that way—don't look at me. I want you to connect even when you can't see me.'

This was more difficult. Without actually seeing the ring on his finger it became harder to visualise the connection. Finally instead of the ring as a whole she started to imagine the intricate filigree design and the image in her mind became clearer; the connection sprang forth.

'*Ahh, got it!*' she thought to him.

'*Okay, now keep the link and keep walking. I want you to weave your way between those crates.*'

As soon as she started to think about her direction, about avoiding the rats and the rubbish, the connection dimmed. She came to a halt, and concentrated hard. It came back to strength again.

'*Good! Good! You didn't lose it,*' he thought to her, '*but you gotta be able to walk and talk at the same time. Have another go.*'

She tried again, and was more successful this time, but each time she had to step over something she found the link weakening and she would instinctively slow her pace. She tried for another few minutes but could not stop herself slowing.

'*Okay, we'll leave it for now. We'll practice again some other day. I'm the one who'll be doing the walking for now anyway. Back you come,*' and he broke the thread.

She was amazed at how tiring the intense concentration was. They sat down on some of the crates for a while and he explained their next move.

'You've probably noticed that we have more than our fair share of pimps and pushers around here. And you'll see a lot of young girls fall victim to it; runaways mostly. Every now and then Nancy and I would try to even the playing field a bit. Send a few of the dealers broke.'

'How?'

'Pinching drugs and drug profits. It's just a matter of tracking your dealer to his lair, pinching his cash and destroying his stash of drugs. Less drugs on the street, less cash to buy more, and often, one less dealer. The smart ones don't stick around after they have been done over. They take to the hills before their boss comes calling for his cut.'

'Do you feel up to it? Do a good dead for the day?'

'Sure. It might take my mind off things.'

'That's the spirit! Hop in my pocket and let's go for a walk.'

Although Tom considered Philip Cole a suspect in the abduction and murder of Rebecca Cole, he was not about to let Philip know that. He would play the sympathetic cop, and let the two constables play the bad cop roles. Then maybe in time Philip would let something slip.

He called ahead, and caught Philip at home before he left for work. Better to give him the bad news at home.

Philip Cole was looking haggard. For a moment, Tom thought his suspicions might be misplaced. Philip waved him in to the lounge… it was a mess.

'Want a coffee?'

'Yeah, thanks; white, no sugar.'

Tom waited in the lounge room, perusing the photos on the mantle while Philip was busy in the kitchen. There were very few of Rebecca. Most were older people—parents perhaps? And holiday scenes. Philip at the Eiffel tower; hiking on a mountain somewhere; relaxing at a tropical bar.

The floor was covered in discarded clothes. Several pairs of shoes and socks surrounded the main armchair, discarded after flopping into the chair to watch TV, Tom guessed. The dirty dinner plates on the side table gave credence to the idea.

Philip re-entered the room and passed a coffee to Tom, slopping a little of his own onto the floor in the process. Philip barely seemed to notice the mess, throwing a tie to one side and taking a seat in his favourite chair.

'You've got bad news, haven't you? That's why you wanted to talk here,' he said quietly.

'Yes. I'm afraid so. We've matched your wife's DNA with that found at a crime scene at the wharves,' he paused and put his coffee on the table. He looked Philip straight in the eye and continued, 'We haven't recovered a body, so we cannot be a hundred percent certain—but, I'm sorry Mr Cole—it seems highly likely that your wife is dead.'

Philip looked at him for a moment and then stared at the ceiling, his jaw clenching. Was he trying to hold back tears?

'If there was no body,' he asked looking down to meet Tom's eye again, 'what did you find that makes you think that she's dead?'

'I can't tell you all the details, it might impact our investigation, but I can tell you that there was a very large quantity of blood. That, and other evidence, confirms that your wife was at the scene and that it is most likely her blood. It was the same blood group. It is very unlikely that someone could lose that much blood and live.'

'But there is a possibility that it's not her blood; that someone else was there too with the same blood group as her?'

Was he avoiding the truth or rummaging for clues?

'A small possibility, yes, but we think it is unlikely. When the final DNA analysis of the blood comes back we'll know for sure.'

Philip nodded glumly and stared at the floor.

'Would… would it have been a quick death?' he asked, eyes intense, searching Hayes' face.

'I really couldn't say Mr Cole. I'm not a forensic scientist.'

Philip was an intelligent man; he saw through it straight away and turned even whiter. For a moment, Tom thought Philip was going to be sick. He gave him a moment to recover himself a little.

'Did your wife have any enemies?' Tom asked, in a quiet, concerned voice. 'Anyone who would wish to harm her?'

'No. No! She was a homebody—a nobody. She never hurt anyone.' He was wringing his shirt in his hands; twisting it back and forward. It would tear soon.

'What about yourself? Is there anyone who would want to hurt her to get at you?'

Philip paused.

'No. I don't think so. We've never had any serious problems with the business; I don't really have any enemies—certainly not anyone who would resort to this! You think someone who knew her did this?'

'We don't know at this stage. It could be that the man who abducted her picked her at random.'

'So what do I do now?' Philip asked in a daze. 'I mean, there's no body. Do I tell everyone she's dead? Do we have a funeral for her? I mean what now, what on earth now?' His eyes were roaming around the room, fixing on the familiar, as if trying to shake himself out of a dream. He was getting distressed, more so than Tom had anticipated. Perhaps Philip had nothing to do with his wife's disappearance after all.

'I'm afraid we wait, Mr Cole. Until we have enough evidence for an inquest to report a finding, Rebecca is in limbo. I would suggest you advise friends and family that it is likely that Rebecca is dead, but there is not much else that can be done at this stage.'

Philip dropped his head into his hands.

'I will let you know as soon as we have any more information. Will you be alright Mr Cole? Is there anyone I can call to come and sit with you for a while? Friends, family?'

'No. Thank you, but no. I think I'll just sit here for a while,' he said rubbing his face and staring at the floor.

'Would you like me to call your office, let them know you won't be in?'

'Yes. Yes, that would be good. Thank you.'

'Okay. Well I'll leave you for now then, but call me if you need to talk, or if you think of anything that might be of interest. I'll see myself out.'

Philip nodded again and watched him leave the room. He looked numb.

Tom wasn't sure what to make of that. He had fully expected the guy to put on some kind of crocodile tears, but Philip was obviously in shock. If it was an act, it was award winning. When he got back to his desk he rang Philip's office and told them Philip would not be in. Philip's business partner said he would check in on him later.

Philip was squeaky clean so far, no convictions, no arrests, no suspicions, not even a bloody speeding ticket. One of two architects in a partnership, good steady work but nothing awe inspiring. Married five years ago to Rebecca, no previous marriages, no children, small mortgage outstanding on their inner-city townhouse, no other debt, good income, good credit rating. No signs of any gambling, drug or alcohol problems, and no life insurance policy on Rebecca. If Philip was the guilty party, money didn't seem to be a motive.

Philip had called Rebecca a 'nobody'. Well as far as her records were concerned, Rebecca really was a nobody. A birth certificate, a marriage certificate, a driver's licence and a Medicare card were her only identity records. No criminal records, no passport and no property ownership. That was unusual. The house and both cars were in Philip's name only, yet both had been purchased since their marriage. An old-fashioned marriage perhaps?

A quick check of her tax records showed she'd worked for the same company for the last eight years—probably since she left school.

He found the company's phone number in the directory and made an appointment to see the head of staffing the next day. They may be able to shed some light on things.

Time to delve deeper into Rebecca's private life; maybe she had a shady side.

She bounced about in his pocket as he walked. He had made a small hole for her to peep out of and by holding on to the sides of this she managed to stay upright as he trundled along. As he walked he sent his thoughts to her, describing the people they passed and what he knew about them. Some waved or nodded in greeting. He was well known in the area; that much was clear.

Finally they came to a dingy café and the old man ordered a coffee and a plate of fish and chips. He sat at a table to one side where he could clearly see everyone coming and going.

'This is drug central,' he thought to her, *'deals going on here all the time.'* She looked around, but she couldn't see what he meant at first. There were lots of people coming and going. Handshakes. Cars pulling

up outside and people leaning into windows, lots of SMS conversations. And then she noticed a flash of white powder as a small bag was passed from one hand to another. Coloured pills in another. Unless you were looking for it, you wouldn't even notice. He slipped a small piece of chip into his pocket for her.

'*Most of these guys are small fry. Not worth even bothering with. The big guys are a lot more subtle. You see the two guys up near the counter? They are the dealers. Cash coming in, drugs going out. At some point one of these guys is going to run out of something and will have to restock. When that happens he will send a message to the boss and arrange a pickup,*' he thought nodding towards the large tattooed man at the counter.

'*When he runs out this guy will lead us to the supplier. There are probably bigger fish above the supplier, but he's got enough drugs and cash to keep trade going down here for a few days at least. So, up for a little fun?*' He thought to her.

'*Sure. What do I do?*' she replied.

'*For starters, when he leaves you, follow him—travel size, with your glow dimmed right down. Make sure he doesn't see you, and follow him to the supplier. Then you follow the supplier and find out where he is operating from. If you get the chance, you pinch as much of his cash and drugs as you can. If it's too risky, you just come back to me with the details, and we plan something for later. In order to pick up the money, you will need to return to full size, which is why you don't do this unless it's safe. You cannot risk being seen. You got that?*'

'*Sure.*'

'*In time, I'll teach you how to change the size of other things without changing your own size at the same time. But that will take a lot of practice.*' He thought to her. '*So for now we wait. He may have people to see when he leaves here—you may not meet the supplier for some time. You can still talk to me even if we are miles apart. You just have to concentrate harder. So, if he's dilly-dallying, try and send me a message, let me know you're still on the trail.*'

A customer approached the dealer and after a brief conversation, left again empty handed. The dealer had started texting. She watched the man as he punched away on his mobile phone then placed it on the counter. A beep; Mr Tatts checked his phone and then ambled towards the door.

'*Off you go. Don't lose him. I'll wait for you at home.*'

She shot off like a rocket, slipping through the door before it closed, and almost running into the back of his head. He had stopped to talk to an old lady outside. She zipped up into the awning above the door. A moment later he broke away and continued down the pavement, strolling quickly towards the main shopping centre.

He stopped at a park bench and sat down next to a man in neat white clothes; she guessed he was a hospital wards man. The wards man was eating his lunch and reading a novel; they ignored each other. There was a laptop bag on the ground next to him. Mr Tatts sat down, and leaned back casually on the bench. He sent a few texts and then, a moment later he picked up the wards man's laptop bag and walked away! Had he just stolen it? Then she realised that there was a second laptop bag behind it. Before she could decide whether to follow Mr Tatts or not, another man came and sat down. When he left, the second bag went with him.

So, the wards man was in the business.

A few minutes later, he got up, dropped his rubbish into the bin and walked away. His phone beeped from time to time, and he deftly keyed messages with his thumb as he walked. It looked like business was booming.

She followed him to a dingy pub called "The Rose and Crown" where he met up with a tall rough-looking man (who looked vaguely familiar to her for some reason). She could not hear much of the conversation as they kept their voices low, but she worked out that Mr Business was in fact called Bill. Unfortunately, she never heard the name of the man she recognised.

Bill finally left the pub and after a short walk, entered an apartment in an upmarket part of town. He let himself in and dumped his wallet and keys on the kitchen counter and plugged his phone into a charger, and then he moved into the master bedroom. He pulled the curtains shut and made a quick check of the room. Satisfied, he slid the wardrobe open and pulled the clothes hanging inside away from the wall. She watched him from the light shade as he pressed on the wall and a panel popped open revealing a narrow doorway. The space revealed was large enough for him to walk into, and she guessed that originally it had been a built-in wardrobe facing into an adjoining bedroom. He pulled a light cord, illuminating several shelves that were neatly stacked with small plastic containers filled with pills and powders. A small safe was bolted to the wall at one end; he opened this and stashed the cash from his pockets inside. From the glimpse that she got of its contents, there were thousands of dollars inside. On another shelf sat a plastic container filled with small snap-lock bags. He filled several of these with a selection of pills. There were two laptop bags on the floor. He grabbed them both and tucked a selection of pills and powders into each, and then he closed up and left the apartment.

She watched him walk down the street from the window, and did not return to full size until she was sure he was gone. She was surprised to find that she was strong enough to slide the wardrobe door open. She made her way into the wardrobe and pushed the cupboard door open. She pulled down hard on the light cord and it came on. The safe was closed. Why bother to put the money in a safe if it's already hidden in a secret room? She turned the handle, hoping that he hadn't spun the dial, but the safe was locked. Should she take the drugs? If she didn't take the cash as well he would just buy more, and he was going to know someone had been there so there would be no chance of coming back later. But they may not get another chance; it seemed a pity to let the opportunity go to waste.

She pictured Andy's ring in her mind and concentrated hard on its design, and slowly, slowly, she felt the connection emerge.

'Andy? Andy, can you hear me?'

'Yes, I can hear you. Where are you?'

'I'm at his apartment. He has a secret room. I can get to the drugs, but the cash is in a safe and it's locked.'

'Okay, we might still be able to do this. You sure he'll be gone for a while?'

'Well he loaded up with more drugs.'

'Probably a good sign. Okay, we'll try this once, but if it doesn't work I want you to get out of there, and leave everything as you found it.

'I want you to place your hands on the lock and think about the metal wheels inside.'

She followed his instructions and was surprised to find that she could visualise the mechanism inside.

'Can you see it?' he asked.

'Yes. What do I do now?'

'I want you to turn the first wheel to the right until you see it click into place. Then when you've got that one, do the next one in the opposite direction until it clicks too. Keep alternating directions until you've got all of them in place. Have you got that?'

'Yes, and I've got the first one.'

There was a noise; a key in the lock.

'He's back!'

She quickly shrank and jumped into the plastic container holding the snap-lock bags, and wiggled her way underneath them. She could just peer out of the side of the container.

The light!

She threw a desperate thought at it and, to her surprise and relief, it went out. But the door was still open, and so was the outer wardrobe door. She heard his footsteps in the kitchen, and a bling of a mobile phone being unplugged from a charger.

He forgot the phone. Maybe he would leave now.

'What's going on?!' Andy was whispering in her mind.

She was afraid to respond in case she accidentally made a noise. She was trying to hold her breath so she could hear what was happening in the kitchen.

The steps started for the door and then stopped. A moment's hesitation; then they started coming back toward the bedroom, the sound becoming muffled once he stepped onto the carpet in the hall outside the door. The bedroom door was open.

There was no noise.

Where was he?

She couldn't see any part of the bedroom from where she was hiding, only the inside of the cupboard and part of the wardrobe it was hidden in.

She strained her ears. Nothing. She began to doubt her own senses. He left and she hadn't heard him? No. She would have heard his feet on the tiles. Something had alerted him.

She was struggling to breathe quietly.

'Renee! Are you OK!' Andy sounded desperate.

She decided to take a risk, even if she did accidentally speak aloud, it should be too quiet for Bill to hear.

'I'm hiding. I'm OK. Can't talk, have to listen.' She mentally whispered.

'OK.' Andy replied. She could detect his mental sigh of relief.

There was still no noise from the hall or the room.

What was he doing? Waiting? Searching for an intruder?

The minutes dragged by and she felt like her heart would explode.

Bill's face appeared around the edge of the cupboard door, and her body jerked involuntarily from the surprise.

He did not notice her.

She heard him exhale, and he slid the gun in his hand back into the holster hidden under his wards man's uniform.

He entered the cupboard and turned on the light. He tried the safe, it didn't open. Thank God she had only cracked the first wheel.

He was so close. She could smell his sweat and hear his breathing, still heavy from the excitement. Bill twirled the combination and opened the safe, taking the cash out and checking it before replacing it and locking the safe again. He took down a container of pills stacked right next to the bags she was hiding in and she ducked for cover. She listened, holding her breath as he pulled each container off the shelf and inspected it.

Finally, he stood back and surveyed the entire scene.

His face was puzzled.

He reached out, his hand stretching out to the container she was hiding in, she couldn't move, he would see her. He plucked two zip lock bags from above her, only one concealed her, the double layer of transparent plastic providing only a hazy cover for her.

She held her breath, could she make herself smaller? She whispered the spell in her mind and imagined herself the size of an apple seed.

She felt sea sick, all she could see were the white walls of the container and the semi-transparent bag pushing down on top of her, its weight suddenly much more than it had been. She felt like she would be crushed. There was a kink in the plastic to one side of her forming a tent and she wiggled her way over to it. She could breathe again. She had never had such a terrible feeling of claustrophobia before.

Above her mega Bill was loading pills into the plastic bags, completely oblivious to her. His breathing sounded like a hurricane, and the sound of the containers being placed back on the shelf beside her was like cannon fire; the whole shelf vibrating and knocking her of her feet.

The room went dark.

A boom signalling the closing of the cupboard; a metallic sliding sound as the clothes were slid back to cover it and a muffled slide and bang as the wardrobe door was closed. A distant thump was perhaps the bedroom door. She could hear no more.

Desperate to escape the stifling plastic she transformed to fairy size and climbed out of the container, gulping deep breaths of air.

She heard the front door slam.

She flew over to the door and pushed it open.

She slipped between the hanging clothes and moved the wardrobe door just enough to squeeze out. She checked the entire apartment. He was definitely gone. He had taken his phone this time and there were no other items on the kitchen bench.

She returned to the cupboard and to human size.

'Andy, I'm OK. He's gone. He didn't see me.'

'Just get out of there. That was too close.'

'No. He has definitely gone this time. I can do this.'

'Renee!'

She cut him off.

She wanted to do this, and she was not going to let him or fear stop her.

She went back to the safe and slowly worked the wheels of the safe until each clicked into place. The handle moved and the door opened.

She loaded a garbage bag from the kitchen with the cash and another with the drugs. She closed everything up and turned off the light, leaving everything just as it had been. That would give him something to think about.

Fingerprints didn't matter; she had never been fingerprinted; besides she was dead now. She shrank and was glad to see the garbage bags shrink with her. She left the flat and flew back home to Andy.

She sat at the kitchen table with Andy and sorted through the booty. She had scored over $50,000 in cash.

'What do we do with the drugs?'

'Burn 'em. Not here though. There's a glass works not far from here that keep their furnace running all the time. Once they shut down for the night, you fly in there and chuck 'em in the furnace and they burn up in seconds.'

'So what are we going to spend all this money on?'

'Food, a few house improvements, and a new identity for you.'

'How will we get that?'

'This will probably come as a surprise to you,' he said dryly, 'but I know a few shady characters.'

Changeling

The next morning after breakfast, he drilled her on all she had learnt, making sure she could perform all the incantations correctly. She had been practising whenever she could, afraid that she would forget something, but she was also beginning to enjoy her new skills.

'Okay, well you've remembered all that, I think it's time to try hiding your wings again. You definitely know how to use them now so that should help. But first, I think we'll need a mirror.' He disappeared up the hallway and came back soon after with a full-length mirror mounted on wheels.

'Same principle as changing size. You need to picture yourself with wings and without wings in your head. We'll use the mirror first, then you'll need to learn to do it with your eyes closed.'

She stood before the mirror.

'Now, do you remember the words?'

'"Foe-lay" to hide and "Foll-she" to reveal.'

'Good. Okay, whenever you're ready.' He went and sat in one of the dining chairs to watch.

She concentrated hard on the pattern of her wings, on the structure, on the colour and then imagined them fading away as she said the word.

Nothing happened.

She tried again. Still nothing.

She turned to him, exasperated.

'I don't understand it,' he muttered. 'You've got the words right, I know you can feel your wings, and you're getting the shrinking thing right with no problems at all. I'll have to do a re-think on that one.

'Well. Let's see how you go changing your appearance. No words for this one—it's all in your head. Look in the mirror. Now I want you to think yourself blonde.'

She did so and was amazed to see it happen immediately.

'Ahh. No problems with that one at all. So I don't know why you can't do the wings.

'Never mind. Now—go berserk. Hair, eyes, nose, mouth—play to your heart's content, and don't worry that you won't be able to go back to normal. The normal shape is what your body knows and wants— you'll find you sort of default back to that without even trying. It takes an effort to stay in a form that isn't natural to you.'

She turned back to the mirror. She turned her hair black, grew her nose and covered herself in witch's warts. This was incredible! An imitation of Marilyn Monroe came next, followed by Angelina Jolie. It was surprisingly difficult to get the features right from memory, but she got the overall effect right. Then she tried an old bald man, a punk with blue hair and finally settled on a black haired Asian girl.

'How's that?'

'Fantastic. Actually, the one you're doing now—remember that one. I think that will be a good look for your second ID. Unfortunately, it means we will have to pin your wings down somehow when we do the ID photos.

'I'll have a think about that too. The sooner we get it done the better.'

Berry's transport was an old family company, and it had resisted the trend of outsourcing the office staff. All the staff were housed in the one large depot together, and as a result, each had a fair idea of what went on in the other parts of the business.

The head of staffing for Berry's Transport, Mrs. Nora Hodge was a grey-haired lady well past accepted retirement age. She shook Tom's hand and showed him into her office. She gestured Tom to a seat, and took her own place behind a desk stacked with papers.

'How can I help you? It's about Rebecca Cole isn't it? Her husband rang to see if she had contacted us, and then I saw the news the other day. Is there any word?'

'Nothing concrete yet, I'm afraid. We are worried about her safety, so any information you can provide might be of help, no matter how insignificant it seems. She has worked here for a number of years I understand?'

'Yes. She went off on maternity leave last month.'

'She's been here for…' he flicked through his notepad, 'at least eight years if my information is correct?'

'Yes, that's right. She knows the job inside out. We are holding her position open for her.'

'She was a valued employee then. Did she have any enemies here?'

'No. Everyone loved Rebecca.'

'I need to get some background on Rebecca, anything about her friends, her family, anything that might shed some light on things. Firstly, how well do you know Rebecca?'

'Oh, we were reasonably close—for co-workers. I think she related to me in a mother/daughter sort of way. Advice; sounding things out, you know. I've known her since she started here; before she married Philip.'

'Do you know Philip?'

'No. I've spoken to him on the phone a couple of times, but I've never met him. He was never interested in meeting any of Rebecca's friends—always too busy. But I know a bit about him, Rebecca talked about him a lot. He's a bit of a control freak I think.'

'In what way?' Now he might be getting somewhere.

'Well, she had been supporting him for the last God knows how many years through university, and helping him get a loan to buy his share of the partnership with that other architect. But every time she wanted something for herself, he always said they couldn't afford it. When it was something for him—well that was another matter. She had wanted a car of her own, but he refused to let her have one, said they couldn't afford it. And then when they could afford it, there was some other excuse. Then one day he decided it would be much more convenient for him if she had her own car—so he went out and bought one for her in his name. A bloody great four-wheel drive, so he could use it on the weekends when he went off-roading with the boys. Didn't ask her what she wanted, just went out and bought it, and then made her pay to run the damn thing. She was livid. If I was her, I would have refused to drive it, but she always gave in. Well I couldn't understand why she put up with him, but she loved him, and she said he was just trying to make her happy.

'But she finally stood up to him when she got pregnant. She refused to have an abortion, and when he still didn't want anything to do with it, she moved out. It was rather good timing, her inheriting the unit off her auntie.'

'I thought she was renting the apartment?'

'No, she got it a couple of months ago. It probably hasn't been transferred to her name yet—it was taking her a lot of time to sort through all the legal stuff.'

Tom was scribbling madly.

'That must have been a sizable inheritance; it's prime city real estate. Do you know what Philip's reaction was to her inheriting the place?'

'Well, she told him she was leaving before she told him about the inheritance, and when he found out about the apartment he said if she divorced him he would get half. Well she expected him to try that, so she had already been to see her lawyer and she was able to correct him straight away. It was left to her, not to him. There is a caveat in her aunt's will apparently (she was a canny old biddy) saying that it was for Rebecca and not Philip, and if they were ever to divorce, it would not be counted as joint property. Anyway, he wasn't very pleased about that. He had a major tantrum.' She paused for a moment.

'You know, everything that Rebecca has told me about Philip over the years has made me think he is a narcissistic, selfish, son-of-a-bitch. But, honestly, I can't help feeling that he doesn't have anything to do with her disappearance.'

Tom nodded, being an arsehole didn't necessarily make you a murderer.

'Rebecca was starting to get a bit suspicious of Philip with money though. She suspected he was skimming money from his pay before she saw it, putting it aside for his own little luxuries, and then playing poor when the bills had to be paid.

'The other architect at the firm let something slip in front of her, made it sound like Philip was on a lot more money than she knew.'

Well that was definitely worth looking into. Maybe Philip had a habit of some kind after all.

'Thank you for your time Mrs. Hodge.'

'Please let us know if anything...' she trailed off. Tom suspected she didn't want to finish the sentence.

'Yes. We will.'

He had one more person he wanted to speak to today, but it was going to be a challenge. Babayaga didn't speak any English and he suspected she was a little bit crazy. The warehouse was in her territory. She might have seen something.

He found her seated on a park bench not far from her usual haunt. She lived in the park, and had done so on and off for as long as he could remember. He had spoken to her before, so she knew he was a policeman.

'Hello Babayaga.'

She gave him a smile and patted the seat next to her. Many people thought she was from Russia, but she had told him once, through an interpreter, that she was really from Estonia.

She called out in Estonian to a young woman seated under a tree.

The woman came over and sat next to her. After a whispered exchange the young woman turned to Tom.

'Babayaga says she is always happy to have a handsome man come and sit with her, but today she also has something to tell you.'

He laughed. 'Please, go on.'

'Rebecca Cole is dead.'

Detective Hayes looked at her surprised.

'Why do you say that?'

Babayaga waited for the translation and then replied.

The woman translated again.

'You don't know for sure, but you think so don't you.' Babayaga was looking at him intently.

'Me? Personally? —most likely. But there isn't enough evidence one way or the other to support that.'

Another brief exchange in Estonian, then—

'No, I understand, you don't want to upset people before you're sure. But you see… I know she's dead… I felt her die. It was about 2pm on Tuesday 17th. I feel these things sometimes.'

Surprised, Tom checked his notes. She was within the ballpark.

Tom wasn't one to believe in hokum, but he wasn't going to dismiss anything that might give him the edge on an investigation either. She could be using this as a bizarre cover story to hide how she got her information.

'Did you sense anything—any details apart from her death?'

Babayaga looked at him with surprise, and then a smile appeared. He had obviously won some brownie points for hearing her out.

'Well. I think they killed her and took her baby, and I think the baby is still alive,' the interpreter said. That stopped Tom short mid scribble. He stared at her and then at Babayaga.

'What makes you say that?'

The interpreter waited for Babayaga to finish and then continued, 'Well. It wasn't like other deaths. I'm old, I've felt quite a few in my time. This was… weird. To start with, I could feel one ball of energy, Rebecca, and she was dying. She was in terrible pain and she was terrified.' Babayaga was holding back the tears that threatened at the corner of her eyes. She spoke again and the woman translated, 'then I could feel two, which is when her baby boy arrived I think, then I felt Rebecca die, but not the other.'

Tom continued to scribble for a while.

Babayaga looked at him intently and continued. 'Do you plan on telling your colleagues any of this?' the interpreter said.

'Not in so many words; but I am going to suggest that they investigate certain avenues.' This whole thing was getting weirder.

Babayaga nodded. 'Wise move,' her interpreter translated.

'Let me know if you think of anything else.' He said passing her his card. 'Thank you both, you've given me lots to think about.'

He was drinking coffee at his desk, going over his notes again. Maybe it was time to take a chance and start looking for the baby. It was an unlikely story, being murdered for your baby, but he knew it had happened before. What was the woman's name? She was American. He did a Google search on the internet.

To his surprise, three references came back, not one. Three times? That it could happen once was horrific enough, but three times? And now maybe four.

He flicked through the file to the record of conversation between Constable Peale and Mrs. Cole's doctor.

Peale had remembered to fill in the phone number at the top of the form—good lad!

After a couple of rings, the phone was picked up.

'Doctor Trent's surgery.'

'This is Detective Inspector Hayes; could I speak to Doctor Trent please?'

'One moment and I'll see if he can take your call,' the phone switched to on-hold music abruptly.

A moment later, there was a click and then a cultured voice came on the line.

'Doctor Trent here.'

'Detective Inspector Hayes here, Doctor Trent, you spoke to one of my constables, Constable Peale a few days ago about Rebecca Cole?'

'Yes, yes, I remember; dreadful business. She'd be just about due by now poor woman. No luck yet I take it?'

'No, I'm afraid not. I wanted to ask about the baby actually. Did Rebecca know what the sex of the child was going to be?'

'Funny you should ask that, she did, but she didn't want to know.'

'Pardon?'

'Well, when I got the results back from the ultrasound, Rebecca and her husband came in and I asked them if they wanted to know the sex. Rebecca said no, and her husband said yes. Which I thought was a bit odd, since he had already said he had no interest in the child at all. So I asked Rebecca to leave the room and I told him it was going to be a boy. Then he got up and told to Rebecca to come back in and as soon as she sat down he told her it was a boy. Laughed his head off. Complete effing imbecile if you ask me. Excuse my language, but civil words completely fail me in his case.

'I asked him to leave. I also advised Rebecca not to bother bringing him to any future appointments. He was obviously too immature to be of any assistance to her or the baby. She was much better off without him.'

'That seems to be a recurring theme.'

'That does not surprise me in the least.'

'Thank you very much for your time.'

'Not at all. Such a lovely lady, I do hope she turns up safe and well soon. Good day.'

As soon as he finished the call, he went to missing persons to register one potentially missing baby boy.

The Burning

Andy opened the package and spread the contents on the dining table. There were two photographic driver's licences, two Medicare cards, two passports, two birth certificates and a selection of other useful paperwork for both identities.

Renee Roswald, daughter of Andy Roswald was the one she would be using. She had changed her green eyes to brown for the photo and changed her long auburn hair to a light brown colour in a short, cropped style. It was an easy transformation and she did not have to think very hard for it.

The other set was in the name of Anne Lin, first generation Australian of Chinese parents. They were her backup, in case she really needed to disappear.

So she was Rebecca Cole no more. He had taken her to a photo booth, crouched behind her and held her wings down while the photos were taken. An easy solution for what they though was going to be a difficult problem.

'We need to find a safe hidey-hole for this second set. The rest you'll be using as your own from here on in. Well, as soon as we can work out how to hide your wings. For a while there I was starting to think it's because you aren't Sidhe. But then, why would you still be able to use all the other magicks and not that? So I just don't know. Maybe I've got the words wrong? I am an old man after all. We'll work it out eventually. It doesn't matter at the moment.'

'Is this how Nancy remained hidden? Using fake IDs?'

'No. She never bothered with any of this. She just stayed away from the authorities and kept her head down. The people around here knew she was my wife, but they kept to themselves pretty much. But times are changing. Everything is monitored. If you get caught up in something and you can't provide ID these days, they take you in as being a suspected terrorist or an illegal immigrant or something. Much safer to have some decent documents. These ones will check out OK on the police database if they do a search.'

'Now, we've still got $40,000 cash left. You take ten, I'll take ten, we'll put ten away with the other passport in case of an emergency and the balance can go on some home improvements I think.

'Next question is—where are we going to hide our emergency stash?' he said looking around the room. 'It needs to be somewhere we can get to it in a hurry, but not easy for anyone else to find.'

'Well, I can shrink it can't I? So we can put it just about anywhere.'

'Good thinking! We'll use one of Nancy's old handbags.' He put the cash and the passports inside a red clutch purse.

Renee stared at the purse and willed it to shrink. It shrank to the size of a pellet of chewing gum.

'How did you do that?' Andy asked her in amazement.

'I just thought about it, the same as I did with my face.'

'Good gracious me! I thought you needed special faerie words to shrink things. Can you shrink yourself that way—without the words?' he asked her.

She gave it a try.

It worked.

She increased her size back to normal again.

'You didn't need the words to grow again either?'

'Nope.'

'Wow. All the other faeries have to use the words—or it doesn't work. Very interesting. Let's tuck this little purse inside the telephone for now.' He flipped the cordless handset over and tucked the miniature purse into the battery compartment beside the battery.

'Easy to grab the phone and run if we have to. Now, I need to meet my old mate Bruce for a drink. I have been putting him off for weeks. Are you going to be okay by yourself for a few hours?'

'Of course, I'm not exactly sixteen am I!'

'No! I didn't mean it like that. It's just you have to be careful so as not to be seen. If those bad faeries come calling, or you need me for something—just think to me and I'll get back as quick as I can.'

'Okay dad. Quit worrying and go and enjoy yourself.'

He chuckled as he let himself out.

It felt a bit strange being alone in the house. She was at a bit of a loss as to what to do with herself.

She wandered into her bedroom and sat on the bed. The mirror was standing in the corner. She started pulling faces and making her eyes and nose stretch into incredible grotesque forms.

Stop it or the wind will change and you'll be stuck like that forever, she thought to herself. Her mum used to say that. She couldn't picture her mum, but she could almost hear her voice as she thought the words.

Suddenly another thought struck her. If I can change my face, and shrink a purse without magic words—why can't I shrink my wings the same way? She rose and stood before the mirror. She turned so she could see her wings and willed them to get smaller. They started to shrink. She kept going, the excitement rising. Soon they were like tiny leaves sprouting from her back. She made them smaller still until they were only just visible. A new thought occurred to her—could she change them into something else? What about a couple of moles? She concentrated and sure enough they changed into tiny brown spots.

A woman with two small moles on her back was much less noticeable than a fairy with wings. She changed her eyes and her hair to match her passport.

She could go wherever she wanted now.
No one would know that she wasn't human.

She wondered for an instant if she should try to change her wings back again, to make sure she could if she needed to, but she suddenly had an overpowering desire to get out of the house, to move among people again.

She grabbed a coat and some of the cash and went out to hit the town!

Mr. Manny had been surprisingly accurate with his description of the bald abductor. Tom had an enlightening conversation with a member of the drug squad, followed by a search of the database of known drug offenders, and had found a potential match. Mr. Manny had confirmed he was their man from a photo. William John Bryce—a nasty piece of work with a string of minor drug charges and assaults to his name. Part time bouncer, part time mechanic, and ready for any dodgy work with a nice pay packet.

So, a piddling little drug courier branches out into abduction and murder. To Tom, it stank of a hit, and Mr. Cole certainly had motives, but somehow, it didn't fit. Philip Cole had been visibly shaken when he had told him it was likely that she was dead; and almost ill at the thought it could have been prolonged and violent. So far they hadn't found anyone else who hated Rebecca enough to kill her. Perhaps it was about stealing the baby after all?

The drug squad was keeping an eye on Mr Bryce, and passing on any interesting tid-bits that might help the investigation into Rebecca Cole's murder. The more charges they could get him on the better.

Andy wandered down the road and entered "The Contented Soul". It was an old English-style pub wrapped around the corner of a triangular shaped building. He nodded to the bartender as he made his way along the bar towards the tables near the front window. Bruce was already seated gazing out the window with an empty glass in front of him.

'Too dry to wait for you, you slow old bastard,' Bruce grinned at him as he came over. 'What kept you?'

'A woman in need.'

'Ha! You lying old drunk—when's the last time you've had anything to do with the fairer sex?'

'Well, I assume you'll have another then, while I tell you a fine faerie tale?'

'Too right.'

Andy trudged up to the bar and ordered two schooners of Guinness. Leaving the money on the counter and the bartender to the slow task of filling them, he slouched back and dropped into a chair. He leaned back, shooting Bruce a sly look. Bruce knew it well.

'You weren't kidding were you?'

'Nope.'

'Here?'

'Yep.'

'Shhhheeeee-it. It's not…it's not Lucy, is it?'

'No. By god, I wish it was—but no. But who knows; maybe this one can help me find Lucy someday.'

'She's not one of them is she?'

'Nah. She doesn't know who she is. Neither do I. I know most of the old legends, thanks to Nancy, but this one's got me stuffed,' he said as the bartender brought over their creamy brown glasses.

'Ta Bob,' said Andy as he scooped up one of the glasses and

demolished a quarter of it.

'You guys sharing fairy tales again are you?'

'Aye,' said Andy dragging his best Scottish accent back from the grave. 'Tradition.'

'Tradition! You do realise you're drinking Irish beer in an English pub in Australia?' the bartender remarked, laughing at him.

'Every tradition starts somewhere,' he replied with solemnity.

Bob retreated to the bar grinning. He was always happy to serve them, they were a couple of mad old buggers but they always paid and never caused any strife.

Once he was safely out of the way, Andy continued.

'The warehouse. It was her that was killed. She came back as a faerie somehow.'

'Bull shit.'

'Nope. I saw her body.'

'Bull shit,' he said again staring Andy straight in the eye.

'Nope.'

'Humans can't become faeries! Never heard of such a thing. Abducted by, murdered by, cursed by faeries—sure no argument. Become a faerie? No.' Bruce argued downing another draught.

'I agree—I've never heard of such a thing. But I saw her body with my own eyes, and now, the body is gone and here she is before my own eyes—a faerie.'

'A changeling. Looks the same—isn't the same,' he said with warning. 'How do you know it isn't that old witch Clio in disguise? She could have taken the body and taken on her looks.'

'Why would she do that?'

'Who knows why faeries do anything they do?'

'True. But I feel it in my heart that this is not the case. This one is a lost soul.'

'Be… so… very …careful …Andy.' Bruce said leaning forward across the table towards him. 'You know more than I how bad things can become.'

'Aye. I will. But there's more; and I will need your help…'

She walked down the street, peering into the shop windows and was constantly surprised by her reflection. *My God, I really do look different—and human*, she kept thinking.

In a jewellery shop she found a beautiful classic-styled watch with a leather strap. She took it to an engraver and had a message inscribed on the back.

A new dress and shoes to match came next and then a lobster dinner with champagne and butterscotch pudding for dessert.

She ambled home and went into her room to try on her new dress and shoes. She felt alive again. The shop had gift-wrapped the watch for her and she left it sitting on the dining table for Andy to find when he came home. She tucked a note under it to let him know where she was going; there was one more thing that she wanted to do tonight.

She had been thinking about the day she stole the money and drugs from Bill, and the image of the man that he had met in the pub kept coming back to her. She was sure that she knew him, but she could not place him. Now she decided to try to find him again and see what she could discover.

She needed to be in miniature again for this, and at first she was reluctant to give up her new found human form. Looking like this, she could pretend to be a normal human for the rest of her life; live like a normal person. Except she already knew that this was impossible. She wasn't going to age the same way as a human. If she tried to live a human life, she would have to keep disappearing or pretending to kill herself off; starting again as a new person in a new place. Her blood, her hair, her skin; all of these were different. If she became ill and was sent to hospital—what would happen to her when they realised what she was?

No, she could never live as a human; she could only make brief excursions among them.

She flew back to the Rose and Crown in miniature and snooped about. She saw plenty of other low life, but not the man she was after. She circled the streets in the area, looking at all the people who passed.

A couple of hours later, when she was about to give in, she spotted him arguing with a man in a suit outside a restaurant in China town.

'You're crazy. I am not paying twenty grand for damaged goods!' said the suit.

'Okay, okay, I can accept that. What will you pay me?'

'For that, nothing! Do you honestly think my wife is going to accept it in that condition? Forget it. The deals off. You'll have to find somewhere else to offload it.'

With that, the man in the suit stormed away and the tall thug swore loudly. When he moved on she followed him. She could still not place him.

He started punching numbers on his mobile phone as he walked. She could not hear the other side of the conversation.

'The fucking deal's off. The little prick doesn't want shop soiled goods.'

Another pause, then 'Yeah, I know, I know! Do you think I'm happy about this? Look we'll find someone else okay, and then he'll get his cut; it just might take a little longer than I hoped.'

He listened and then ended the call, swearing loudly as he shoved the phone in his back pocket.

He walked a long way, finally entering a mechanics workshop by the office door. She slipped in behind him before the door closed. He went through the office and into the workshop. It had a very high ceiling with wooden rafters supporting a corrugated iron roof. She positioned herself up on one of the beams to watch. There were two other men in the workshop, eating takeaway at a card table. They were familiar too. One was bald and solid, the other thin and fidgety. There were several cars in pieces and the whole place smelt of oil and kerosene.

He approached the table and started yelling at the bald man. 'You do realise you've just pissed twenty grand up against the wall don't you?'

The bald-headed man flushed with rage and stood up pointing his finger threateningly at the newcomer.

'Oh nooo. You can't pin this fuck-up on me,' said Baldy, approaching the first with menace.

'There was no way that little cock-sucker was going to pay twenty grand for damaged goods,' yelled the first man.

'Well if you'd kept the fucking chloroform happening she wouldn't have been jumping around like a jack rabbit and I wouldn't have cut the little fucker would I?!' the bald man replied, moving threateningly towards him, his voice rising.

'Will you two shut the fuck up? The little bastards quiet for once—do you want it to wake up?' said the third man through gritted teeth.

All three glanced over to the box near the old meat safe.

'Okay, okay' said the tall one raising his hands. 'So where do we find another buyer?'

'Look,' said the third man standing up and moving between them, 'I'll talk to my contact tonight, he might be able to find us one.'

'Well it better be soon 'cause I can't stand the fucking noise, or that pong, for much longer. Besides, some bastard will hear it and start making trouble,' said the bald man as he moved back towards the table.

She could not see inside the box from where she was so she flew over to a beam above it. The baby was a new-born. His hands were tiny. He was so beautiful. One tiny arm was heavily bandaged. Blood had seeped right through the gauze.

She knew without touching him that he was dead.

And that he had been hers…

The whole horror of her death came flooding through her mind in an instant.

She knew what they had done to her.

She remembered the paralysing fear.

She remembered every struggle, every punch, every cut, every scream.

She struggled to stay upright.

And then the rage hit her like a bomb blast.

She appeared full size beside the box and lifted the child into her arms, turning and directing the full force of her rage at the three men staring at her.

There was a heat so intense she felt her skin tighten; a light so brilliant and white she feared she would never see colour again. The whole world became a white, boiling void.

Slowly the world and her breathing returned to normal. Normal; except for the greasy scorch marks and the three piles of ashes smoking in the middle of the floor. Their shoes were strangely unaffected by the blast.

It had been very quick.

Not like what they had done.

She held the little body close to her and returned to miniature. She was about to leave when there was a knock at the door. She froze. A second, louder knock.

'Police. Open up.'

She flew up into the rafters again and watched as the police opened the door. Three of them filed in, handguns ready, eyes scanning the place.

'He's around here somewhere, I saw him come in.'

They all came to an abrupt halt when they saw the burn marks and the shoes. The smell of burnt flesh was incredible.

'What the …?'

'Tom! What the hell is that?'

'Leave it! Check the place out first—they might still be here,' he said dragging his eyes away from the smoking carnage and covering his mouth and nose.

She watched them as they did a quick search of the place, and suddenly realised that she was not alone. Somewhere in amongst the rafters, another fairy was hiding. She turned suddenly, sensing it behind her.

It darted down towards the door, a pink light, not green. It pressed against the door and the door opened enough for it to slip out unseen by the police.

The police had finished their search and returned to the mess in the middle of the floor. She decided it was time to leave and made her way over to the door. She dimmed her glow as much as possible, but one of the officers still managed to catch sight of her and stared at her curiously. It was the same cop that had seen her at the warehouse. She turned up the intensity of her light so that all he would see was a tiny ball of light—no features. He followed her as she made her way to the door, pushing it just enough to squeeze through.

'What the hell was that?' she heard one of the others exclaim as she disappeared out the door.

Forensics were going over the scene; photographing, labelling and sweeping up the ashes into sterile containers.

Tom and the drug officers were outside sitting on a low brick wall getting some fresh air. The whole thing was beyond weird. There were a couple of stolen cars, partially stripped and in the process of being reborn, and a few thousand dollars' worth of neatly bagged drugs ready for distribution. Since the perpetrators themselves appeared to have been incinerated, the drug squad were rapidly losing professional interest. Personal curiosity was another matter entirely.

None of them had been able to explain the green light or what they presumed were the ashes of the three gang members. Not even the most advanced flamethrower could have achieved that. What exactly were they dealing with?

Mysteries aside, the item that had attracted Tom's attention was the cardboard box they had discovered in the old meat safe. It was lined with blankets and there were a couple of large bloodstains on them. A dog bed or a makeshift crib? Blood tests on the blankets would be able to establish whether or not it was human blood. But he was pretty sure he already knew. The question was, where was the baby now, and was he still alive?

The other fairy was gone. She could not sense her anywhere.

She needed somewhere quiet, where she would not be disturbed. There was a house nearby—its occupants were out somewhere for the night; she was beyond wondering how she knew that.

She commandeered their bathroom, filling the bathroom sink with warm water. She washed him, handling him gently, cleaning the gash in his arm cautiously as if to prevent further pain. He was so perfect; tiny fingers and toes. His eyes were closed. She would never know what colour they were; to open them—unthinkable. The child she had spoken to day after day, sung to and planned for, while it snuggled in her womb; how could this be happening? She never got to hold him and feel the warmth of his skin and the gentle snuffles of his breath…

She could not bring him back. That was impossible. She knew it in her bones.

She wrapped him in a towel. Clothes, a nappy, a baby blanket; these were the things she needed now.

A children's clothes shop was easily entered. She took a plain white christening gown, a white cloth nappy and a baby's blanket. Money left on the counter for payment.

There was a couch against one wall for customers and she gently laid the baby down; she did not have time to grieve yet.

This would be her first real nappy change, practised so many times at pre-natal classes. How ironic it should be so neat and perfect and yet so utterly unnecessary. She had dreaded the thought of endless dirty nappies, but now that this was the only one she would ever change, she would give anything to have that burden back. This piece of cloth was irrelevant now, useless, yet somehow, he would seem uncared for without it.

He was clean and dressed and swaddled; safe from the cold he would never feel. He was ready. She cradled him in her arms and locked the shop door behind her.

A picture on a telegraph pole stared at her as she left the shop. Her own face was looking back at her. Rebecca Cole. It should be so important to her, but it seemed meaningless. What did it matter anymore? She still had little memory of the person that she used to be…

A sudden flash of memory—

Philip, her husband; kissing her on their wedding day. Holding hands as they walked along a beach in Fiji—their honeymoon. Drinking champagne at the opening of the architectural firm with his business partner. Warmth and love and hope.

Their home; it is dark, a lamp only partially lighting the room. She is seated on the couch; he is standing in front of her:

'We agreed on this years ago—no kids!' He is standing over her, hands on hips.

'Yes, but that doesn't change the fact *that I am pregnant.*'

'So what?' he said, voice raised.

'So, I am pregnant. This isn't something I can wish away, and anyway, I don't want to. I want this baby,' pleading.

'It's the hormones talking,' angry and dismissive.

'No. I want this baby.' Firm.

'I don't. This wasn't part of the deal. Get rid of it.' Walking away, discussion over; marriage over…

She stood shaking for a moment, the small cold child clutched in her arms. He didn't want the baby and he didn't care how she felt about it. He didn't care about her at all.

A twitching feeling at the corner of her mind alerted her to the fact that Andy was trying to connect. She shrugged it off and the connection dissolved. A momentary guilt. No time now, he would have to wait.

High on a mountain surrounded by thick bush she found a suitable site. The stars were beautiful here, and the sound of a nearby waterfall calmed her. She placed her baby on a soft bed of ferns and made sure he was tucked up in his blanket. Then she completed her next task. Once that was finished she flew back to the centre of town.

The young minister had just locked the church doors after the evening service when she appeared before him. He had no time to voice his surprise before she had her arm around his waist and he had become as small as a fly.

'Don't worry, this won't take long. I'll bring you back safe and sound.'

He was too stunned, hypnotised by the scenery flashing past him, to do anything but groan.

She deposited him on a rocky outcrop on the side of a mountain.

'Wait here, I'll be back in a minute.'

He stood dumbfounded. It wasn't a dream. A fairy had just abducted him. He was a modern minister, he didn't believe in angels, spirits or devils in a physical sense. He had always argued that the bible used these things figuratively. He certainly didn't believe in fairies and goblins. His whole ideology had just been turned upside down and given a really good shake. He had to laugh—then he had to stop; it was too shrill and unnerving.

She returned with a small bundle, and guided the minister by the hand to a mossy clearing near a waterfall. There was a small hole dug near a beautiful flowering tree. His heart sank.

There were tears in her eyes.

'I need you to conduct a burial service for my baby.' She gently removed the folds of the blanket from around the child's face. He was so tiny. The minister nodded.

'Does the child have a name?'

'Yes, James Cole.'

'Will the father be coming?'

'No.' That was it, the tears started.

The minister was sympathetic. He made it short; an appropriate reading and a prayer. When he finished, she kissed the child and covered him carefully in a blanket. A small bunch of wildflowers was placed on top him and together they carefully filled the little grave with earth.

'I'll take you back now.' A pause… 'Thank you.'

Back at the church, when she made to go, he said, 'If you need anything… someone to talk to. I'm right here.'

'Thank you,' she said, touched.

She flew back to the grave. There was a large smooth rock near the waterfall that made a suitable grave stone. Once she had positioned it on the tiny grave she finally let the memories and the grief come crashing down. She did not move for two days.

Christmas Beetles and Tiny Feet

Tom was sitting with his feet on the desk and a notepad across his knees, gazing out the window. The afternoon sunshine was warm on his face, and was highlighting the few strands of red in his otherwise brown hair. It was a beautiful day and the colours reflecting off the windows of the building across the road were mesmerising him. A flash of green amongst the pattern of light drew his attention back to the issue he had been pondering.

What on earth had that green light been? He had seen it twice now; once with the drug dealers at the garage and once at the warehouse. There were fire flies out west in the rain forests, but he had never seen one anywhere near the city. Perhaps it really was an exceptionally beautiful and luminous Christmas beetle. A quick search of the Internet had not found anything of any use—plenty of weird stuff though.

The weirdness of the whole thing made him think of his conversation with Babayaga. She was definitely a weird old biddy, but at the same time, he had a sense that she wasn't as big a nutter as their conversation should have suggested. Three piles of ash on the floor were acting as a wedge, pushing the door of his mind open. Whatever happened there, it wasn't normal, or natural, or immediately explainable. Perhaps the forensic guys would come back with a logical explanation, but his gut feeling was that the case would be left open.

While he was mulling this over, George, one of the forensic officers from the Crime Scene Services Branch, came in with a bundle of photos.

'Check this out and tell me I'm not going mad,' he said passing a large photograph to Tom. It was a pool of red liquid with two clear red barefoot prints emerging from it.

'Looks like footprints to me. Where was this taken?'

71

The photographer passed him another larger photo. It was of the inside of the bloody warehouse. Tom stared at it.

'What? I didn't see any barefoot prints there—only shoe prints. Where were these?'

'See this bit here,' George asked pointing to the bottom of the larger photo. There was a string of tiny dots emerging from the pool of blood. 'I thought I'd see what kind of insect made the marks. What can I say—I like bugs. This is a blow up of that.'

Tom stared at him, and then back at the two photos. A second look at the smaller photo of the footprints revealed the size of the floorboards and nails in comparison to the footprint.

'This is a joke right?'

'Nope. Take a look for yourself,' he said and passed Tom a magnifying glass. There was no mistake. Even in the larger photo, using the magnifying glass, they were discernible as human footprints.

'Have you shown these to anyone?'

'No man. This is too freaky.'

'Don't. Not yet. This case is getting weirder by the minute. This has got to be some kind of setup—maybe a signature. This could be a key piece of evidence if we find the bastards that did this.'

'My lips are sealed. I'll leave these with you,' he said, 'got other fish to fry.'

'Thanks George.' He stared at the footprints. They looked like a woman's—probably too delicate for a man. He tried to judge the height of the woman based on the size of the prints. About an inch high would be his guesstimate.

Christmas beetle size.

Andy opened the front door and closed it quietly behind him. Conscious that Renee may already be asleep; he slipped his shoes off and left them by the front door, padding down the hallway in his stockinged feet.

Her bedroom door was open, and he realised the room was empty as he passed. All of the lights in the house were off. A slow unease began to build in his stomach. Where was she?

He turned on the kitchen light and immediately saw the present on the kitchen table. The note underneath was of greater importance to him, and he read it quickly. Relief and worry washed over him in turns.

She had gone out. She had managed to disguise her wings. She wanted to find a man from a pub…

It was after ten and she wasn't home. She had failed to mention what time she left or when she was planning to be home. No mention of the name of the pub either. She was a grown woman, capable of looking after herself, but he couldn't help feeling like a worried parent; helpless, staring at clock, waiting for a rebellious teenager to come home.

He put the kettle on and sat down to wait, turning the present over and over in his hands mindlessly until the scream of the kettle jolted him back to his senses. Cuppa made, he sat down and finally paid attention to the gift. He tore the paper off carelessly. He was not really interested in the gift; he would rather Renee was here safe at home. The box inside was fancy; from an upmarket jeweller. He was surprised and delighted when he opened it to see a simple, silver watch with a strap of textured brown leather. It was well made, elegant and sleek. He turned it over and saw the inscription on the back:

'To Papa Andy, love Renee.'

He felt his eyes well with tears and wondered at himself; brushing them away hastily lest she return and find him blubbing like a fool. He was surprised at the strength of his paternal feelings for her, and how quickly she had become an essential part of his existence. Perhaps she was a partial salve for the loss of his daughter, Lucy.

And then of course, variations on a worried parent's thoughts started to crowd his mind and fight for attention:
Has she been caught?
Was she in trouble?
Has she been hurt?
Has she been killed!?
Does she need help?
She isn't ready to be out on her own yet…

But reason eventually held sway again and he remembered to try the ring. He sat perfectly still and concentrated, attempting to make contact with her mind. The thread of thought snaked and shimmered in his mind, but instead of winding out into the distance, it drooped and faded like smoke from a dying fire.
She was not accepting the connection. Why!?

He got up and paced the room.
Was she asleep?
Was she dead?
Did Clio have her?

Maybe she just wants some privacy. He sighed. He wasn't her dad. She wasn't a child. He sank back down into his chair again and sipped his cooling tea.

All he could do was wait.

The sun shone in through the kitchen window and found an old man with a stubbly chin slouched in a kitchen chair. It seemed an impossibly uncomfortable position to sleep in, but a tired body and mind are capable of amazing feats of impossibility.

It was the light shining in his face, rather than the stiffness of his joints, that roused the scruffy fellow, and he was momentarily at a loss as to where he was.

A second later his mind was fully alert. He dragged himself up and checked the bedroom along the hall. No change. She wasn't home.

He needed a shower and a coffee. He needed to think.

Twenty minutes later, he was dressed, caffeinated and heading down the road to Bruce's place. He was halfway there when a poster on a shop wall caught his attention. Renee stared out at him.

Rebecca Cole. So that was her name, he would have to remember that, he didn't have a pen and paper on him. He read on. She was pregnant when she disappeared. Only a few days away from her due date...

The body, the blood, the bundle; they had killed her and taken her baby.

Oh my God.

He sat down heavily on a low brick wall.

He was still there twenty minutes later when Bruce came wandering down to the corner shop.

'Andy? You 'right there, matey?'

Andy looked up at him, face pale, and pointed at the poster. 'It's her.'

Bruce turned his attention to the poster.

'How can that be her—it says here she was heavy pregnant?'

'They killed her for the wee baby, Bruce, for the baby.'

Bruce stared at him and then back to the poster.

'I saw them leave the warehouse with a bundle.'

'Oh Andy…' Bruce sat down heavily beside him. 'Are you sure it's her? What sort of monster must they be—to do such a thing?'

'It's definitely her.'

Bruce looked back to the poster again. Such a pretty young thing; how could anyone do that? Then a thought struck him. 'Does she know yet, Andy? Has she seen this?'

'I don't know. She went out last night. She hasn't come back. Bruce, I don't know where to look. What if…'

'Don't you be starting that—d'you hear me! What ifs will be the death of you. We'll work something out. We'll find her.

'Come on, I'll get you home, you need to be there when she comes back. I know some folks, maybe they've seen something.'

He helped Andy up and guided him back the way he had come.

A couple of hours later, Bruce knocked on Andy's front door.

Andy was there in a second; he had been pacing the floor waiting for him.

'Anything?' he asked, taking a seat at the kitchen table.

Bruce placed a plastic shopping bag on the table and pulled out a bottle of Scotch whiskey.

'Not good then…' he said, standing up to retrieve two glasses from the cupboard.

'Oh Andy, I don't know what you've got yerself into this time,' Bruce said, dropping down into a chair and pouring them both a good measure. 'Where do I start?'

'Is she alive?'

'I don't know. Probably. But I don't think you need to worry about her too much, Andy, she seems to be well able to take care of herself.'

'What do you mean?'

'I think she found the baddies; the ones who killed her.'

'And?'

'They won't be killin' anyone else.' Bruce downed his drink in one go.

'Tell me everything.'

'I went to Babayaga.'

'My God, is she still around. I thought she would have kicked off years ago.'

'Yeah. She's still going strong—and she hears everything. The coppers don't realise she can speak English. She says that there were three guys working at a car repairers place, the one in the old meat works on Butcher's Lane. She was in the lane when the coppers raided the place, but they were too late. Somebody beat them to it. They had to sweep the three of them up with a broom; ashes and shoes—that was all that was left.'

'No…' Andy said, eyes wide, 'that's not possible. I have never, ever, heard of a faerie being able to do that.'

'No, me neither, but it must have been her. Babayaga said they had a baby with them, and they were going spare; they were arguing about the crying—and the baby was gone when the coppers arrived.'

'She didn't see Renee?'

'No, but then, she wouldn't, would she? You taught Renee how to fly and what not, didn't you?'

'Yes.'

They both refilled their glasses.

'Are you sure she's telling the truth?'

'Well, I went past the garage and the cops have got it taped off. That cop that questioned me at the warehouse was there—the tall guy; couldn't get within three feet of the place.'

Andy nodded.

'What now?' Bruce asked.

'I don't know. Wait and see if she comes back I suppose.'

'Are you sure you want her to?'

'Yes.' He had no doubts about that. Whatever she was capable of, yes, he wanted her to come home.

Memories of Philip

It had taken him days to arrange the work on the flat. Luckily, he knew a builder capable of keeping his mouth shut. The drug cupboard was being converted back to its old wardrobe status, and a new hidey hole was going to be built in his other apartment. The one he held in a false name.

He didn't like being without a nest. Carrying this much cash and dope around on himself or in his car was just plain dangerous, but he couldn't afford the down time. He had been running around like a blue-arse fly for days, and now he had to waste time on these three amateurs. They were supposed to call him days ago.

He was a block away from the garage when he noticed the cop car parked out the front. He drove straight past noting the police tape across the front door from the corner of his eye. He continued on for a couple of blocks and turned the corner, parking in the carpark of a hardware shop. What the fuck had happened now? Those muthers still owed him ten grand for their last consignment.

He needed a new hammer. The last one had been discarded, along with some scalp and brain matter, so he went into the shop. He selected a nice heavy claw hammer with a rubber grip—easier to hold in slippery situations—and sought out the most talkative of the checkout operators.

He handed the hammer to the boy taking his time to extract the money from his wallet.

'What happened down the road? Been a murder or something?'

'Yeah, three men killed by the look of it. My uncle's a cop and he said they were fried to a crisp. Reckons they were in with the mob or something, stolen cars and such, but I dunno. I think he's havin' a lend of me. They used to come in here all the time for stuff, and they seemed alright to me, just a bunch of mechanics.'

'Yeah you're probably right. Start thinking like a cop and you'll suspect everyone of bein' a crim. Maybe I'm an axe murderer—oh sorry, make that a hammer murderer!' he laughed, and the boy laughed with him.

'Yeah. Load of old bollocks I reckon,' said the boy. 'Probably just an argument over a car that's got heavy or something,' he said, feeding the money into the till and passing Bill his change.

'Yeah, you're probably right,' Bill said.

'Hava good day.'

He walked back to his car, threw the hammer on the passenger seat and sat down in the driver's seat.

'Fuck! Fuck! Fuck!' He slammed his hands on the steering wheel with each curse.

That bunch of fucking meat heads had probably cost him ten grand and now he had to find another distributor for this side of town. He pulled out his mobile phone and punched in a number. The kid could have it wrong, but it didn't really matter, whatever it was that had happened, this particular franchise was out of action.

At least it would be very unlikely that it would be linked back to him.

'Bill here. Got a problem at the garage. Sounds like the three mechanics have been killed and the cops have the place taped off.' He paused, listening then added:

'Nah, looks like we're going to have to treat the whole thing as a write off. As far as I know they hadn't off loaded it, besides, the stupid buggers kept all their proceeds on the premises. Still, they might not have found the safe—I will get someone to have a look.'

Another pause.

'Yep. I'll get them to keep an eye out and move in once the coast is clear.'

He ended the call. The dumb shits probably had the cash and the drugs in the back room if they got hit during the day, so he would probably be paying to bust an empty safe. Still— it had to be worth a try. Ten grand was ten grand, and if they had managed to sell the kid there could be another twenty grand in there.

He picked up the phone again.

'You up for a job?' A pause.

'Now. Surveillance to start with,' another pause.

'Meet me at the local in ten.'

He finished the call and threw the phone on the front seat, starting the car and heading off into town.

She had cried herself out. She felt tired and weak. She was tempted to just lie there forever, but her stomach was grumbling incessantly. Her beautiful new dress didn't look so crash hot anymore. It was covered with dirt and leaves and she'd torn it in a few spots on the bushes. She didn't really give a damn. She headed home.

It was late. Andy was sitting on the couch, a corner lamp lighting the room. He turned his head when he heard the front door open.

'You're back... I was getting worried,' he said quietly, 'I've been looking for you everywhere.'

She sat down on an armchair opposite him.

'So you found them,' he said.

She looked up at him surprised.

'News travels fast around here—especially about strange stuff like that. Word is... the cops had to sweep them up with a broom.'

'Why didn't you tell me I was capable of that?' she said intensely, straining to keep control.

'I didn't know you were. None of the others are.'

'Then what made you think that I did it?'

'Revenge.'

'Revenge for what?' She got up and walked into the kitchen. How much did he know? How much had he known all along—how much had he kept from her?

'You aren't a normal faerie; you weren't born into the Sidhe,' he said following her. 'None of the normal rules apply to you. I saw your body, I saw what they had done to you...' he stopped suddenly, turning away.

She stared at him.

'Did you know there was a baby?'

He spun around again, aghast. 'No! God no! It was dark, I saw them leave the warehouse with a bundle, I had no idea what was in it! I didn't even see their faces. After they left I found your body.'

'How did I become this...this *thing*?' she said, her voice full of bitter disgust.

'I don't know. I don't know,' he shouted waving his hands in the air. 'I got the hell out of there as soon as I could. You were dead; there was nothing I could do!'

She turned her back on him, angry and sad and afraid all at the same time.

So he hadn't witnessed her death or her rebirth.

He was just an old man who had been in the wrong place at the wrong time.

She sighed.

He wasn't the enemy.

She would still be hiding in the workshop if not for him.

None of this was his fault.

'Nancy couldn't do this—this fire thing—she would have told me,' he said shaking his head. 'The faeries will know by now—they'll be scared.'

'Yes. One of them witnessed the whole thing I think,' she said turning back to face him.

'One of them was at the old meat works?' he asked sharply.

'Yes. I didn't sense her until it was over.'

'They might try to kill you,' he said sadly. 'You don't obey the rules, and now they will know that they can't *make* you either.'

Yes, she thought. They know my strength now. They will never accept me even if I wanted to join them.

They both stared at the floor, lost in thought.

Finally Andy roused himself and asked her:

'What are you going to do?'

'I don't know.'

'Did they still have your baby?' he asked her, breaking into her thoughts.

'Yes… But he was dead. If I'd found him earlier…' and suddenly she was angry at him again. If he had told her what he knew earlier she might have tracked them down, she might have found her baby while he was still alive.

'How could you have found him?' he said, 'I didn't know who your killers were until after you'd killed them. It was only after they were dead that all the crap started floating to the surface. I had no faces and no names. How could we have tracked them down? They might as well have been invisible,' Andy said, walking over to her and placing a hand on her arm. 'None of this was your fault. There was nothing we could have done. Those bastards got what they deserved.'

She slumped in defeat. She wasn't sure how she felt about anything at the moment.

'Oh… thanks for the watch,' he said quietly.

She could not sleep. Images kept crowding her head. She tossed and turned. She kept pushing them away, but they kept coming back.

She had just buried her child, possibly the only child she would ever have. That she and her husband would ever have. Did he really not want the baby?

Maybe that memory was just how he had felt at first? Maybe he had changed his mind as the pregnancy progressed?

Where was he now? Was he worried about her?

She had to know. Was there a future there with him?

Where did they live?

An image of a town house with a neat little front garden came to her. She knew where it was. She didn't even consider what she was doing; she just went.

First his place gets done over, now this. He couldn't help feeling that something strange was going on. He slouched into the lounge chair, and put his feet on the coffee table. He thumbed the buttons on his mobile; maybe his man in the force would know something.

'It's me. What happened at the Garage?' Bill asked him.

'I was there, and I swear I have never seen anything like it, you are gunna think I am a madman if I tell you.'

'Tell me everything, doesn't matter how mad it seems. There is something fishy going on. What did you see?'

'The three goons; all that was left were burnt shoes and a pile of ashes. The homicide guy who was with us was very interested in some bloody rags in an old box, but otherwise, the place looked untouched. There was still cash and drugs stashed in the kitchen; no signs of a forced entry; no signs of a struggle. There was a weird green light too. It flitted about like a bug. One of the others said it looked like some kind of firefly on drugs, but we don't get fireflies here, so God knows what it was. It got out the door somehow and vanished.'

'Let me know if you hear anything else,' said Bill.

What the fuck was going on?

She entered the house through a vent in the bathroom wall and flew along the hall and into the combined kitchen dining area. The house was dark. Nobody was home.

She flew onto the light shade. She hadn't really thought about what she would do when she got here. The moonlight shining through the kitchen window was glinting on the specks of silica in the kitchen bench top. She and Philip had renovated the kitchen together, and the sparkly bench top had been the one item that they had been able to agree on.

A sudden memory…

…placing a shopping bag on the counter.

'Where were you?' Philip yelled, 'you didn't take your phone with you!'

'I went to the shop,' Rebecca replied, stunned.

'What! Spending more money!'

'We needed milk.'

'But you didn't think to ask me if I needed anything before you left did you?' he snarled. 'Typical, always spending money on yourself—'

This was so untrue it was like a slap in the face.

'You were asleep,' she said shortly; her anger was starting to get the better of her, 'and the milk was for both of us.'

'Don't you dare yell at me! Without me you'd still be living in that little shit hole of a flat! You'd be nothing!' he said slamming down his coffee mug on the counter, shattering it to pieces and spraying hot coffee everywhere.

'Fucken hell!—now look what you made me do!' He stormed out of the house slamming the front door behind him; leaving her to clean up his mess.

Another memory, jostling past the first…

…helping a removalist unload box after box from the truck into her new apartment; joy at finally being free.

Flashes of argument after argument; trying to dictate to her who she could see and when; hanging up when her friends called; inventing emergencies to prevent her seeing them; telling her what she could and couldn't do.

She roused herself.

The kitchen was a mess; moonlight glinting on dirty dishes stacked by the sink. Spills on the floor; the bin overflowing with cardboard packaging from TV dinners. The lounge room and the dining room were no better.

She heard footsteps coming down the hall and was alarmed that she had not heard the front door open. The smell of fish and chips wafted into the room. Philip was in a suit, but his shirt was crumpled and his shoes scuffed. He looked older; tired. She felt a wave of concern for him, but it wasn't love; not anymore.

He collapsed into the couch and swept aside enough clutter from the coffee table to make room for the paper parcel in his hands. He fished the remote off the floor and turned the TV on. He looked haggard.

She watched him tear open the wrappings and break off a piece of fish. He took a bite, but it was clearly not what he wanted as he threw the remainder back onto the pile in disgust. He placed his head in his hands and began to cry; low, deep, exhausted sobs.

She had escaped this man. She had been glad to be away from him, and yet the urge to appear and comfort him was strong. She couldn't; how could she explain what had happened to her, what she was now? She couldn't trust him.

There had been good times, she knew that, she had truly loved him once, but the bad times were so bad. He had been narcissistic and controlling; emotionally and financially abusive, yet to see him crying like this was more than she could bear. If she stayed here she would do something stupid, something irreversible.

She fled.

For a moment, after the memories had started piling up on her, she had wondered if Philip had been responsible for the attack on her. Now she knew for sure, that he was not.

Discovery

It was after nine when she emerged from her room the next morning. It had taken her a while to get to sleep, but eventually she had resigned herself to the fact that she couldn't change the things that had happened.

Andy was seated at the kitchen table and he rose as she came into the kitchen and tottered to the stove to put the kettle on.

'Cuppa?'

'Yes please.'

He grabbed another cup from the cupboard and placed it near the stove.

'I heard you go out again last night. Are you alright?'

'Yes, and no. I don't know if I will ever be alright again.'

Andy nodded.

'Have you remembered everything, about your past?'

'Bits and pieces. New bits keep popping into my head. I remembered my husband last night. I went to see him.'

'Oh my God. Did you talk to him?'

'No. I just wanted to see how he was. I didn't show myself, he didn't know I was there.'

'How was he... ?'

'A mess.'

'Oh. That musta been hard.' Andy said, filling the mugs with tea and passing one to Renee.

'Yep,' she said.

She took a long sip of her tea and blinked back the tears that were threatening to spill down her face.

'Before I saw him, I remembered that he didn't want the baby; that he had been a monster to me and I had moved out. I wasn't expecting him to be cut up like that. It really threw me.'

'Do you think you will want to go back to him at some point? Make up some story and reappear safe and well?'

'No. As much as I hate to see him this way, I'm not going back to that. The more I think about how he treated me over the years—I feel like an outsider looking in now—I can see all the ways he put me down and shut me up and kept me in my "place". No. I am never going to put up with being treated like that again.'

'In a way, that's a good thing. It would be a very hard to reappear. Finding a plausible tale to tell would be bad enough, but trying to hide your new features from him would be just about impossible. And you just can never tell how someone is going to react if they do find out.'

'There is no way in hell that I would trust him with this secret. Not after the last few months. He'd probably try to put me in a side show to make money if he found out what I could do.'

'You don't think he had something to do with your murder do you?'

'You mean a contract killing?'

'Yeah.'

'No...' she shook her head slowly, 'I mean—he was a bastard—but no. Besides, he was distraught. They were after my baby, weren't they?' she said choking up and turning away. She recomposed herself and continued, 'He was never violent. He loathed violence of any kind.'

'No reason to go anywhere near him?'

'I don't think so.'

They sat and finished their tea.

'Do you want any breakfast?'

'No. I'm not the least bit hungry.'

After a while she turned to Andy, 'What happens to all my belongings now? I left everything to my unborn child in my will, or my sister Prue, wherever she is. He might try to challenge the will.'

'There probably won't be anything you can do about it if he does. You are dead now. You won't need the money anyway; there are plenty of ways to survive with your skills.'

'There are a couple of things I want to get from my apartment, though.'

'OK. Well, I'll have a think about that and we'll go and get them before he gets his hands on them. We'll have to be careful.'

He got up and poured them both more tea.

'You have a whole heap of talents now that you never had before, have you thought about how you would like to use them?'

'What? Like become a fairy super hero or something?'

'Not quite what I meant; but not completely off the track. You can't show yourself, so you can't be a visible, known super hero, but there are ways of doing things discretely; making a difference in small ways. Putting drug dealers out of business is one, but there are other more personal things you can do too. Nancy used to visit the children's ward at the hospital and cure sick children when no one was around.'

'I can heal people?'

'Probably; most faeries can. It takes a lot of energy though—so you have to be careful about when and how you do it.'

'Being careful is your catch-cry isn't it?' she smiled at him.

'Well, when you have to hide something this important, it isn't a bad rule to live by,' he replied with a grin.

'Can you show me how to heal?'

'Sure. My arthritis could do with a blast.'

He held out his right leg, the ankle was visibly swollen.

'You need to touch your patient. It doesn't have to be the injury, but the closer you touch to where you want to heal, the more energy you will save yourself. You don't want to exhaust yourself completely or you won't be able to hide yourself or fly away—very dangerous.'

She placed her hand on his leg above the ankle; she was worried she would hurt him if she touched the ankle itself. Almost immediately, she had a sense of the injury and a feeling of bad energy moving towards her hand.

'I can feel the injury!' she said.

'Very good! You didn't have to concentrate at all! Now—push back against it, like you were herding it back into one spot.'

She imagined pushing the bad energy back into a ball in the middle of his ankle.

'Now you need to find your own faerie energy inside yourself, and let it flow down your hands and into my leg.'

That was easy too—it was like second nature. She let it flow out of her hands and into his leg, a stream of golden energy, and then she surrounded the ball of pain with it. Before he could say a word, she tightened the circle, blasting the pain into oblivion and spreading healing ribbons out over the area affected by the arthritis, removing the inflammation and healing the bones and the cartilage. The joint was as good as new.

'Blimey! How did you know how to do that?'

'I don't know. It just sort of happened, like it was subconscious or something.'

'How do you feel? Are you tired at all? Get up and walk around. Do you feel weak or tired?'

She walked around the kitchen.

'No. I feel fine.'

'Excellent. Just don't try to wipe out someone's cancer in one go, or you will wipe yourself out.'

'I could heal cancer?'

'Sometimes; sometimes they're too far gone. You'd just end up exhausting yourself to the point where you could kill yourself—and they still wouldn't be cured.'

'How can I be an instrument of death and a giver of life at the same time?'

'You aren't an instrument of anything. You are you. You decide how you use the talents you have. Good or evil—your choice.'

'I didn't *mean* to kill the baby dealers,' she said suddenly, with tears in her eyes. 'I *wanted* to kill them, I *really wanted to kill them* for what they had done—and somehow I did. How can you kill someone with a thought?' She was up and pacing the kitchen floor. 'How can wanting them dead make them dead? How do I stop that? How can I stop myself from getting angry and reacting—doing it again! What if I ended up killing some innocent person in the wrong place at the wrong time? How do I stop it?'

'Another ring.'

'A ring?' she said, coming to a halt.

'A ring to control it. If you have it on—you can't do it; you take it off—you can.'

'Is there anything that can't be done with a ring?' She laughed through her tears.

'No idea! You seem to stretch all the rules as it is. You'd better go and lie down on your bed; don't want you collapsing on the floor.'

She walked into the bedroom and lay on the bed, then pulled a hair from her head and drew her fingers down its length like he had shown her before.

'What words do I use though?' she asked him.

'I get the feeling you don't need any words,' he said. 'Just think about what you want it to do and what you want to happen when you take the ring off as you wind the hair around your finger.'

She wound the hair and imagined the ring blocking the pulse within her before it could become a ball of flame. She imagined taking the ring off and letting the fire go in one enormous stream. She also imagined the ring staying a ring rather than becoming a hair again. Then she imagined putting it back on her finger again, and blocking the fire again as she wound the last of the hair around her finger.

The hair became a delicate golden filigree ring. It had a small beetle pattern entwined in the gold.

'Well done. When you wake up, we'll go and test it somewhere quiet.'

She drifted off to sleep.

There was a banging on the front door, 'Andy are you up for a pint? I've got news for you.'

'Best hide for a bit, Renee,' Andy said waving her down the hall.

He opened the front door to find Bruce on his doorstep.

'What do you want ya daft old biddy?'

'I've news for you, and I brought supplies,' he said holding a six pack of Guinness cans aloft. 'I think a private place is better for this; if you get my meaning.'

'Come in, come in. All donations gratefully accepted,' he said holding the door wide and ushering him in.

Bruce sat himself at the kitchen table, while Andy retrieved two schooner glasses from the cupboard. Bruce was casting his eyes about the room.

'My goodness, Andy! You've gone all domestic on me!'

'Ahh well, you have to make an effort when you have guests.'

'So she's here is she?'

'Ah, well, I can't keep anything from you can I?' he said realising how easily he had slipped up.

'You are out of practice Andy. You are going to have to do better than that, especially if you are going to get the coppers involved in all this. They will pick you to pieces.'

'Aye. But I've never had to be on guard with you, now have I? You lulled me into a false sense of security and before I knew it my tongue was acting of its own accord.'

Bruce laughed at him and handed him one of the tins of beer.

'You may as well come out Renee. Bruce, here, is one to be trusted,' Andy said as he pulled the ring pull on his can.

A small glowing green light flew down from the top of the dresser and landed on the table before flitting up again and expanding into a blinding green glow. Renee emerged from the dying light.

'What an entrance! Well done. Can you do bells and whistles as well?' said Bruce laughing at her and raising an empty glass. 'I'd make a toast, but your timing is a bit off, fill that up for me will you Andy?'

Renee blushed.

'Take no notice of him, Renee, he is as jealous as the day is long—what he wouldn't give to put on a light show of his own.'

'You daft old bugger, do I look like a show pony?' he said.

Andy winked at Renee, 'You wouldn't know it by the look of him, but he used to do a cabaret act for the soldiers during the war. Slicked hair and makeup, fancy spangles; even a top hat and tails!' He poured himself a glass and chuckled with glee at Bruce.

'I can't do the high kicks anymore, but pass me some tap shoes and I'll give you one hellava show,' Bruce said winking at Renee.

A bemused smile played on Renee's lips.

'Renee—Bruce, Bruce—Renee; right, formal introductions over; what have you got for us?' Andy asked.

Bruce dropped all the banter and sighed. 'Oh Andy; you are in a fine mess as usual. Your saving grace is that nobody knows you exist—yet. Renee here—or should I say Rebecca,' he said giving her a meaningful glance '— isn't the beginning and the end of this.'

'How do you know my name?' asked Renee, startled.

'Well apart from all the missing person's posters on the street, the talk is everywhere. The guys who did this to you, something fried them to ashes. People in the street know that the mechanics killed Rebecca, and they know Rebecca wasn't the first. This goes much deeper than that. They were drug dealers, killers for hire, pimps, and more recently—baby dealers.'

'Baby dealers...' said Renee.

'Yeah.'

'What the...?' said Andy.

'Prostitutes normally; looks like they had a supply and demand problem...' Bruce said quietly.

Renee turned pale.

'They got their just desserts then, didn't they,' said Andy coldly.

'Agreed; but unfortunately, they were just the small fry.'

'This is an organised thing?' said Andy.

'Yes.'

'How big is it?'

'I don't know yet. But there are several runaways who have disappeared off the streets lately, and it's not just the whores who are getting scared. Babayaga told me a heavy turned up the other day and threatened her; told her to keep her mouth shut.'

Renee was stunned.

'What evidence do you have? We have to go to the police,' said Andy.

'Nothing; at the moment, anyway, are you sure you want to be digging a hole for yourself by going to the police?'

'This isn't just some loser drug addict turning drug dealer, Bruce. This is murder and abduction and probably rape. Of innocents! We fought a war against this shit—remember?'

'*Of course I remember*. But we've done our bit. We are old now, we're not nineteen-year-olds out to save the world.'

'True. But we don't have to be in the firing line for this one, Bruce. We can tinker from the edges—get the information to the young fighters of today. They need a leg up. It's their future that they are creating; not ours. Ours is almost done.'

Bruce looked at him intently. 'There is no guarantee you won't get dragged into the middle of all this. Are you are prepared to take that risk?'

Andy nodded. Bruce looked at Renee; she nodded too.

'We'll keep you out of it as much as possible…'Andy said to Bruce.

'Hold on a minute you!' said Bruce flaring in anger, standing up and placing both hands on the table, '—don't you dare be calling me a coward!'

'That is not what I meant and you—'

'Oh, think I'm too old and stupid do you? Gone senile?' Bruce said in a raised voice as Andy got to his feet glaring.

'Please, please!' yelled Renee moving between them, 'Stop—calm down, both of you!'

The two men squared off at each other and slowly, reluctantly, returned to their seats. Renee pulled out a chair at the end of the table and sat.

'We need you Bruce. We need what you know. Andy didn't mean—'

'And how would you know what he means—' said Bruce.

'Sorry Bruce,' said Andy calmly. 'You have never been a coward and never will be—'

Bruce looked at him in surprise, but it slowly changed to a look of wry scepticism.

'—a Nancy-boy maybe, but not a coward,' Andy continued.

Bruce howled with laughter and clapped him on the back; Andy grinned and poured him another beer.

Renee sighed.

The new hiding place in his other flat wasn't ready yet. He was still dealing out of the boot of his car and he didn't like it one little bit. It was too dangerous to drive the car to work, so at lunchtime he was high-tailing it to a locked garage he was renting and stocking up before running back to the park to make the deliveries. Then it was back to the garage again to hide the cash in an old paint tin at the very back of the top shelf. It was slowing him down. Once the flat was ready, he'd be fine, it was much closer than the garage, but he had no idea how much longer that was going to take.

By the time he got back to work, his lunch hour had been over for some time and he was running out of ways to avoid the boss on the way back into the building. The bastard was keeping an eye on him already for some reason, and he did not need any more grief just now.

Today, feeling particularly pissed off about the situation, he decided it was time for action. He sat on the boot of his car and took out his mobile.

'It's me. Everything is taking too fucking long. The boss is getting antsy and I'm worried he might start paying too much attention to my comings and goings.'

'Don't worry about him,' said the voice on the phone, 'I will get the doctor to have a word with him—your poor old mum is sick again, and you need some space. Chill out. I can deal with him permanently if he gets too nosey.'

'What about the flat and the boys? Have you found out who did it? We can't afford any more losses.'

'Agreed; I am looking into the situation—I will let you know. For the time being, we need to keep things moving. That last little set back has tarnished our reputation as quality suppliers. We need some new younger stock, kept in controlled conditions. By the way, whose stupid idea was it to do a slash and grab?'

'I doubt we will ever know, but whichever idiot it was, he won't be doing it again.'

'Next time you recruit, make sure you exclude all the half-wits. Now go and hunt down some more stock, and for fuck's sake, quit whining.'

The phone went dead.

Fuck!

It was always up to him to keep things moving on the street, to stick his neck out.

Although, at least he didn't have to deal with the cartel. He would end up in gaol or dead if things went wrong; Johnny would fare much worse.

The Thief

Breakfast was over and Andy was passing washed dishes to Renee to dry.

'Well Bruce has given us plenty of hearsay, but we have got precious little in the way of evidence.'

'Surely the police will be able to fill in the blanks? They are the ones with all the resources and access to data?'

'True. But I think they will still need a little help. Especially if we want to speed things up so no one else gets hurt. We don't want them to see you though...'

'One of them has already seen me—twice.'

'What! I told you to be careful; you'll have the cops and the fascist faeries after you!'

'Relax, okay, all he saw was a green light—I wasn't that careless.'

'Okay. Okay...' he said pausing to think.

'...he definitely saw the light?' he continued.

'Yep—he was following all over the place until I slipped away.'

'Maybe we can use you as bait. We don't want them knowing where we live, but if we can encourage them to meet us somewhere else—that's another matter entirely. So now we have to find him,' said Andy. 'Where did you see him last?'

'At the garage.' *Where I burned the baby dealers*, she added to herself.

She was a monster; a monster chasing other monsters.

'Before that, he was at the warehouse. He thought I was a Christmas beetle,' she said.

'Ahh... now there's a thought. Can you do that too? Can you change yourself into a beetle?'

Why not? she thought. She concentrated on a beetle shape and colour and shrank herself into a slightly awkward looking Christmas beetle. The feeling was strange, she was used to the sensation of making herself larger and smaller, but this was new. Her skin felt like it was covered in a crispy and hard layer and her eyesight was broader somehow. Her legs felt stiff and they were hard to move; her hearing was multidimensional, sort of echo-y, but with layers of different sounds rather than one sound repeated. The colour of her beetle shell was good, and the sheen, but the head shape wasn't quite right—it was too long. Overall the effect was good enough to pass as a rather ugly beetle. She would have to catch one and study it a bit closer. It would make an excellent disguise for stalking baddies; or policemen for that matter.

She returned to normal again.

'Excellent,' said Andy, 'that will definitely come in handy.

'You know I'm starting to wonder what your limitations are. You seem to be able to do whatever you can put your mind to.' He looked at her puzzled for a while.

'Nancy once told me that faeries can't create things out of nothing, but that they can pull things from alternate realities. I don't know how that works with transforming things though. Well I suppose the lesson is, if you think of something, give it a try and see if you can do it. You won't know until you try.'

'Well, I better not get too distracted playing with this at the moment. I am going to go for a fly and see if I can find that policeman.'

'See what you can find out about him. We want a policeman we can trust, but even then, I don't want you revealing yourself to him. We will have to play this very carefully. Good luck, and send me a thought if you find anything interesting, or take a photo on this,' he said handing her his mobile phone.

She tucked it into a satchel and slung it over her neck. When she changed back into the beetle, the satchel shrank too. The strap was nice and firm around her upper segment, so she flew out the open front window.

The warehouse was closer than the garage, so she went there first.

The police tape had been removed and the place was locked up tight. There was a 'for sale' sign next to the roller door out the front. She flew onto the roof and looked down through the skylight. The mess had been cleaned up and the entire floor had been painted dark grey. She could smell the paint fumes seeping through the skylight. There was no sign of anyone.

Next, she tried the garage. She approached the building with some trepidation. She had not been back since the burning. She wondered if the smell would still be there. It still seemed like a bad dream; how could she be capable of such a thing; such destruction?

The police tape was still around the building, but there was no sign of anyone outside. She landed on the windowsill and peered through the office window. It was all quiet and dark inside. She moved to the rear of the building and looked for a way in.

The back door was not fully shut. Was someone inside? She flew through the gap and into the main part of the garage. All the half-finished cars were still parked, waiting to be completed. The three stains on the floor made her shiver. She tried not to look at them.

A noise from the room off to one side attracted her attention and she flew over to look inside. It was a bathroom. There were benches down one side and a shower stall and toilet against the opposite wall. There were several pairs of greasy overalls hanging from hooks. Standing on the toilet seat was a man she had never seen before. He was removing the access panel to the ceiling. He reached around inside for a while and when he pulled his gloved hand back out it was holding a bunch of keys. He slid the ceiling panel back into place.

He jumped back down again and moved over to the shower stall. There were old tyres and empty oil tins stacked inside it. It hadn't been used for a long time. The back of the shower was made of cheap waterproof panelling. It was greasy and chipped. He moved the tyres out of the way one at a time and there was a gloinging noise as he kicked the oil cans aside. Once he had cleared some room he climbed into the shower and pulled one of the taps out of the wall; there was no plumbing behind it, just a hole. He inserted one of the keys and twisted and the entire panel pivoted open like a door. Behind it, there was a large floor safe.

Another of the keys was selected and turned in the lock of the safe. Then he bent down and started to turn the dial. She could hear each of the locks fall into place and he pulled the door open.

He chuckled softly to himself as he pulled out several bags of pills and some large bundles of cash. There was also a handful of gold chains and rings. He pulled a black cloth bag out of his pocket and filled it with the cash and drugs, but slipped the tangled pile of jewellery into his own pocket. There were some papers in the safe and he cast his eyes over them. It looked like he was trying to decide if they were important or not. In the end, he threw the lot in the bag. He didn't bother to lock the empty safe, but he returned the shower panel to its original position and put the tap back in place. The keys went into the bag as well.

She was tempted to try and steal the bag from him, but decided instead to follow him and see where he went and who he met up with. The identity of his colleagues might be of more use than the contents of the bag.

She made herself a little smaller and landed gently on his shoulder. Why fly when you can ride? He was wearing a motorbike jacket and the smell of tanned leather engulfed her.

He slipped out the back door and pulled it closed. A high wire fence, topped with barbed wire, surrounded the yard at the back of the garage. He strolled quickly to one of the supporting poles and pulled the wire away at the bottom. A single slit had been cut in the mesh from the base of the pole to about a metre above the ground. He slipped through the gap and let it fall back into place. You would have to know it was there to see the damage.

He walked through the long grass past rough scrubby trees and onto a walking path along the side of a drainage channel. There was a motorbike and helmet hidden under a footbridge that crossed the channel and he mounted it and was away in a matter of seconds. She locked her claws into the stitching of his leather jacket, desperate to hang on as he sped away along the drain. A moment later he turned onto a side road and then onto the main road heading into the city. He reduced his speed to blend in with the other traffic.

She found herself approaching a familiar pub. It was the place where she had witnessed the baby dealer from the garage and Bill, the drug dealer, drinking together, "The Rose and Crown". The pub was as sleazy as she remembered and there were some very dodgy-looking people inside.

The thief parked the bike in a lane way and walked into the pub. She disentangled herself from his jacket and flew onto a ceiling fan. She could see Bill sitting at the same table as last time; he was a regular obviously. The biker removed his helmet and ordered a beer. He looked around the place while he waited, glancing at each person for a moment before his gaze moved to the next. Then he took his beer over to Bill's table and placed his helmet on the floor. She flew over to a light fitting closer to them. She changed back to a fairy for a moment so she could take a photo of both of them with Andy's phone. The police might be interested in those.

The thief slid the cloth bag across the table and Bill slid him an envelope.

'Any problems?'

'Nah. I locked up tight before I left. Good setup. You gunna use it again?'

'Dunno. It'll be too hot for a while.'

So Bill was in this up to his neck! She felt an incredible heat build-up inside her and flow toward the ring on her finger, but there it stopped and slowly dissipated. If the ring hadn't been on her finger...

The temptation to remove the ring was so strong—to blow these bastards to hell! She looked down and realised that her fingers were around the ring, preparing to slide it off. What she was doing? God! She had almost done it again! She put her head in her hands.

She didn't have all the facts—it was wrong for her to assume the role of judge, jury and executioner. Was Bill the boss, or just another stooge? Or was he a cop, deep under cover? What if she had blasted him to oblivion and then found out he was on the side of good? She had to get her shit together.

When she looked back to the table, Bill was gone. Shit! She changed back into a beetle and raced to the door in time to see it close behind him. She buzzed about the windows looking for a way out, but with no luck. Eventually another man entered the pub and she was able to dart past him. But it was too late; Bill had disappeared into the crowd. She flew back to the window of the pub and looked inside; the thief had gone too.

Damn! Where to now?

She kicked herself mentally for wasting an opportunity. Finally, she decided to go back to her original plan and try to find the policeman.

She had no idea which building he worked in, and the garage and the warehouse were dead ends. Where else might he be?

There was always her apartment. At some point the police would go over the place, if they hadn't already. She could remember where it was and there were things there that she wanted. Possessions that seemed to be her only link to who she once was; personal things she didn't want the police or Philip getting their hands on.

And then she remembered the necklace. Her parents had given it to her when she was just a baby. Prue was jealous and always trying to snatch it off her. If Philip got his hands on it, he would throw it away or pawn it.

No, that was not going to happen...

It was the middle of the day and the apartment block was quiet. It was long and low; only two stories high. Hers was on the top floor. It had a tiled roof and she was able to enter through a small gap between the tiles. Once inside the roof cavity, it was easy to enter the house via the bathroom ceiling fan. She did a quick circuit of the house in beetle size to make sure she was alone, and then returned to human size. She felt like a stranger in her own home.

She wandered from room to room, looking over all her possessions. Most of them meant absolutely nothing to her now.

In her bedroom, she opened her jewellery box, but the necklace wasn't there. She hadn't seen it for quite a while. There was another smaller jewellery box somewhere, and she vaguely remembered putting it in that before she moved house. It was probably still packed in one of the moving boxes stacked in the spare bedroom. She had been so busy getting ready for the arrival of the baby, that only the essentials had been unpacked.

She had been so happy when she had inherited this place from her aunt. It had been her escape from a marriage that seemed to turn sour very suddenly. But with hindsight, she could see that it had been sour from the start.

She hadn't meant to get pregnant. A bout of vomiting had upset her contraception. But once she knew she was pregnant, she realised that she really did want to be a mother. Nothing was as important as this, and it even made her ready to stand up in the face of Philip's insistence that he wanted no part of it. That had been an awakening. She realised that all their goals were his goals; all their dreams were his dreams. Her dreams had been gently pushed aside again and again. His view of how things should be had slowly smothered them; replaced them. She had thought her dreams weren't important to her anymore but in reality, they were just lying dormant; not defeated.

She and Philip had discussed the baby several times over the weeks following the discovery of her pregnancy. Time and time again, he told her he was not interested in being a father. Did she realise just how much money went into raising a child to adulthood? Much better for her to get an abortion he told her. He had tried an outright statement of facts; he had tried an appeal to her future career prospects; he had tried highlighting how little time she would have to herself, and he had tried to scare her with horror stories about childbirth. Finally, he went too far, he threatened to have nothing to do with the child, and told her he would leave her if her body changed for the worse after the pregnancy.

She had been trying to work out how to fund her escape from him when her aunt Emily had died. At first it was just another body blow—her last loving relative dead.

But then, the will was read. A small consolation was granted to her; the apartment. It solved her housing crisis.

Then of course Philip started threatening to take it away from her. Thankfully, her aunt had thought of that, and made sure it was left to her in its entirety—not to be passed to him in any fashion. A nifty legal caveat had been applied to the title deed, preventing him from getting his hands on it or any proceeds from its sale.

That had been the final nail in the coffin. Their split was a nightmare of paperwork and financial unpicking, which meant she still had to speak to him from time to time, but she was finally seeing him for what he was, a selfish money grubbing bastard. She wondered why she hadn't seen it earlier. Why she had wasted so much time and effort on him to get so little in return.

Well that was then and this is now, she thought. She had changed her will to leave everything to her child.

I wonder what happens now she thought. There was no way to prove that they were dead. How soon before he launched a legal challenge to get everything for himself. How many of her valuables could she get out of the house before he came to claim them?

She found a backpack and shrank her jewellery box, placing it inside. What next? The antique clock her aunt had given her; she shrank it and tucked it into an inside pocket. Now where was her necklace? She opened box after box in the spare room and finally found the small jewellery case in the second to last box. She didn't even have time to open it when she heard a key in the front door. She threw it into the backpack and shrank it and herself and flew up onto the light shade.

It was the policeman.

The room was still a mess of opened boxes.

She watched him wander into the kitchen and look at the calendar attached to the refrigerator. He paused to look at all the papers stuck to the fridge with magnets. Nothing seemed to inspire him. He leaned against the kitchen cabinets and sighed.

'Christmas beetles, spontaneous combustion and missing babies,' he muttered to himself, 'What am I missing?'

He was a tall, sinewy man, but she suspected he was stronger than first appearances would suggest. He had penetrating blue eyes.

He wandered from room to room looking at things until he finally entered the spare room and came to a sudden halt. He slid his gun out of its holster and examined as much of the room that he could see from the doorway. He turned and glanced at the gap at the bottom of the open door and where the hinges joined the wall, checking for shadows or movement, and then he quickly entered the room and held the gun at shoulder height as checked behind the open door. The curtains did not reach the floor and there were no wardrobes or other hiding places. He relaxed a little and then left the room. She assumed that he had gone to check the rest of the apartment. A few minutes later he walked back into the spare bedroom and surveyed the damage.

'Shit!' he said, and pulled out his phone.

'George, I need someone over to Rebecca Cole's house now. Someone has been in here rifling about.' He left the room and moved over to the front door to wait. She wanted to follow him to where ever he was going next so she needed to get close. She didn't want to become a beetle again, he was already too curious about them.

She made herself and the bag smaller again—smaller than a house fly and flew over to him; landing on the back of his coat.

Her senses were sharper now that she was a fairy. This close to him, she could smell the soap and shampoo he used, but also his own unique smell; his skin and his hair. He smelled nice. But there was something else; there was a familiarity about him. Somewhere, she had sensed this before. It was comforting— like a favourite smell—but it was beyond smell, it was on another sensory spectrum entirely. Was this some new sense? She would have to ask Andy about it.

He started to pace the floor again and she was almost dislodged, making her heart leap. Unfortunately, there wasn't anything she could hold on to. She climbed to the top of his collar and peered over. There was a label sewn to the inside of his shirt so she climbed over to it. By holding onto the label and wedging her feet into some of the stitching she was able to stand fairly comfortably without being afraid that she was going to fall all the way down the back of his shirt.

He continued to pace back and forth.

'How did they get in? Did they find what they were looking for?' he muttered to himself.

George arrived and he explained what had happened and added, 'keep me posted, mate.'

'Will do,' said George, and he left him to do his job.

The policeman left the apartment and walked over to his car. She thought she was going to be crushed when he sat down in the driver's seat and leaned back onto the headrest, but thankfully, she was able to hang on and was safe within the curve of his neck.

Well, she had her most precious belongings and she had found the policeman, so things hadn't gone so badly today after all.

She couldn't see where they were going, but about ten minutes later everything became much darker and she realised that he had driven into an underground car park.

He parked the car and walked to a glass door at one end. He swiped his access card and entered a lobby with a lift. They travelled up in the lift and emerged onto a floor comprised of open plan desks and glass offices. It was lunchtime; there were a few people working here and there at desks, but mostly the floor was quiet. He went into an office, removing his coat and hanging it on the coat rack behind the desk.

As he sat down, she climbed up to peak over the top of his collar. The computer was on, but locked and she watched over his shoulder as he entered his username and password. That could be useful she thought.

She needed to find out who he was, and where they were, so she decided to explore. She hadn't been able to see anything on the way in, so she flew out of his office into the open area to try and get her bearings.

The name on the door of the office was "Detective Inspector Thomas Hayes", and the office number was 351, so she assumed she was on the third floor. A quick look at the directory near the elevator confirmed this. It also gave the building name. She flew over to a window to look for landmarks. She knew this area. They were in Surry Hills. She was confident she would be able to find the building again if she needed to.

She flew back to the office and settled down on the coat rack to watch what he was doing. He was opening some photos—crime scene photos. Suddenly she decided she didn't really want to see this.

She flew over to a bookshelf and started to look at the titles. Mostly they were serious volumes on law and regulations; official looking folders with the police coat of arms and boring administrative titles; but tucked in amongst them were several books on art and painting. That was a surprise. She had even heard of some of these artists—the two Australian Margaret's in particular—Olley and Preston. There was a painting on the wall too. Not a print—a real painting. It was signed 'Hayes'. A relative, or one of his own she wondered? It was a city street scene. The Sydney Harbour Bridge was visible in the distance. It was painted with mostly greys and blues, and it looked like it was very late afternoon; the point where the sun has sunk below the horizon and the long harsh evening shadows have dissolved into a softer encompassing greyness. It was a calm, tranquil painting. She liked it very much.

She turned her attention back to detective Hayes. She needed to know if he was trustworthy. She could probably login to his computer when he wasn't around but she doubted that it would tell her much, and it was likely to have all sorts of protections on it. Would she even be able to login in if he had swiped out of the building, she wondered? Would some kind of alarm go off? She looked at the cables running out of the back of the computer. Could she look into them the same way she had looked inside the safe to unlock it?

She was still small enough that she was pretty sure that he wouldn't notice her if she was careful.

She flitted down to the floor and then around behind the desk. Then she flew up onto the desk behind the computer box. She paused to see if there was any reaction from him. He continued to tap away at the keyboard. She took one of the cables in her hands; she could feel the data moving through it. When she closed her eyes she realised she could reach inside it with her mind—it was like entering a glittering sea of ideas. Words, images, numbers and codes whirled through her mind. It was overload. She felt like her brain would explode. She let go. The mad rushing torrents stopped.

She breathed again.

The question was, could she filter out the things she wanted to know?

She placed her hands on the cable again; frantically building a mental wall to block all the images. Her breathing strained, and her body tense. Eventually the rush stopped.

She imagined Detective Inspector Tom Hayes in her head—his name and his face. Then imagined a crack in her mental wall and imagined syphoning off a bucketful of glowing data from the stream of information. The images that came to her now floated into her consciousness at a much slower pace and she was able to look at each one and remember it before it dissolved into another. Hayes as a young recruit, his first arrest, bravery award, promotions, becoming a DI, investigations, and even personal information—where he lived, his marital status, his associates, relatives and interests all flowed through her mind. Hidden deep under layers of security that she could crack with a mere thought were details of a police corruption case where he had been a whistle blower. Those in charge had been able to protect his identity and prevent repercussions inside and outside the police force. One youthful episode of insubordination was the only black mark against his record. From all she could see it looked like he was an honest cop.

The office outside was starting to fill up again, and she began to get nervous, fearing that she would be seen. Now she had his home address, it was time to do some snooping there. She landed on the bookcase again and put the backpack down beside her. If she was a beetle, would she be able to carry the bag with her mouth? She imagined herself as a Christmas beetle again, but this time with aggressive pincers. She trundled over to the back pack and grasped the shoulder straps with her pincers. She fluttered just above the shelf to test her grip on the bag. All was good, so she left the office and flew towards the lifts.

She landed on a light fitting and waited. It wasn't long before the doors opened and someone emerged. She darted in and positioned herself on the edge of the false ceiling inside the lift. There were two others inside the lift, busily consulting their mobile phones. They had not noticed her. The lift went up a couple of floors and the two men got out. When the doors closed she darted down to the buttons and pressed the one for the ground floor with her bottom. Her strength was not in proportion to her size; she was much stronger than a normal beetle.

When the doors opened again she flew out at ceiling height, to make sure she wouldn't collide with anyone. There were glass doors leading out onto the street. She waited for a woman to enter and then flew out above her head.

The policeman's house was in Leichhardt, not far from where Renee's grandmother had lived. The whole area had been made up of single-story terrace houses at one time. Now they had been demolished to make way for modern apartment buildings. Her grandmother's house had been one of them; sold off and demolished after her death. She could still remember the long dark hallway leading form the front door all the way through the house until it met the kitchen and the bathroom at the back. It had been a small, dark, cramped house, but as impractical as it was, she had felt a surge of remorse when she learnt of its demise. There had been good memories tied to its bones.

She found the street easily enough, but the numbering was all over the place. She finally found a small crescent with the same name as its parent, and in it there were a cluster of frightened looking terraces, overshadowed by the enormous apartment buildings towering beside them. His house was one of these. It was a neat and tidy single-story terrace house with cream coloured wrought iron lacework around the underside of the veranda roof. Its corrugated iron roof was painted a dark green. There was a wrought iron fence out the front painted the same green, and the path to the front door was made of red and green and cream decorative tiles—chipped and worn, they looked like they were original. The house itself was a red brick and there was a decorative lead light window above the front door. She was a beauty.

Renee easily entered the house via the eaves, darting under one of the corrugations in the roof and entering the ceiling space. The exhaust fan in the bathroom proved to be the easiest way to enter the house and she left her bag inside the roof to retrieve later. She felt a moment of guilt, intruding on his privacy in such an underhand way, but she had to know more about this man. Before she could put her trust in him, she needed an idea of who he was, and there was no time and no means of obtaining that in a normal way.

She did a quick scan of the house to check that no one was home. She noticed the keypad of an alarm next to the back door. She hadn't thought of that. As a beetle, she should be small enough not to set it off, but there was the possibility of CCTV cameras as well. She would have to stay disguised and do the best she could as a beetle.

There were three bedrooms; one had been converted to a study, another held an easel and painting materials. A large canvas was resting on the easel and several photos were pinned to a board propped next to it. The painting was in its early stages; the scene sketched out in pencil and the sky and foreground completed in flat colours. The photos showed different views of the docks and the wharves along the harbour; one showed the old warehouses crowded along one of the wharves.

The master bedroom was relatively bare; a bed (with a tangled mess of sheets), bedside table, lamp and wardrobe. No paintings or decorations; a pile of books collapsing into a tumble beside the bed.

The lounge had a fairly involved entertainment system and a large collection of music and DVDs. It was tidy.

The kitchen was clean and looked after; cook books standing in a row on a shelf above the workbench and a varied collection of pots and utensils hanging from hooks on either side of the stove. Fresh herbs sat in a jar of water on the bench and the smell of basil and coriander wafted towards her.

She went to his study to see if she could access his computer. It was on and filled the room with a dull hum. She found the cable leading to the computer box and gently pressed her beetle claw against it until she could feel the surge of power moving along it. Once again she let the data flow into her head. This time the torrent was not as overwhelming, she supposed because it was just one computer and not the entire police network. She browsed its contents, searching for anything of interest. There was police casework, financial files, digital photos, and email. He was involved with the Police and Citizens Youth Club from time to time and was a casual member of the local art society. There were emails to and photos of various old girlfriends, but nothing current. It looked like he was living the life of a bachelor at the moment. There was nothing else of any value to her.

She had just flown into the kitchen again when she heard a car pull up in the lane way at the rear of the house, then the sound of an automatic garage door. If the house had a garage, she hadn't noticed.

She flew up onto the top of the kitchen cupboards. Moments later she heard a door close and the sound of footsteps heading towards the back door. A key in the lock and the door opened.

Detective Inspector Thomas Hayes checked the status of the alarm and punched in the deactivation code. He threw his bag onto the couch and dumped his keys into a glass bowl on the kitchen counter. He inspected the contents of his fridge and sighed.

It was late Friday afternoon, he was tired and had no desire to cook, especially not to try and get creative with the limited contents of the fridge. He hadn't had a chance to go shopping and there was no way he was going to do it now.

There was a wine rack built into one side of the kitchen cabinets and he pulled a bottle of red from its depths and opened it, pouring himself a large glass and returning to the issue of dinner.

Water was put on to boil; tinned tomatoes, bacon, garlic and fresh basil were converted into a pasta sauce with ease. Spaghetti was thrown into the pot and Parmesan cheese was grated into a neat pile. Fifteen minutes later he took his wine and dinner to the dining table and retrieved some documents from his work bag and began to mull them over.

She moved to his shoulder so she could read. It was a forensic report from her death. She was fascinated and repulsed at the same time. She got through the first paragraph before she had to stop. *How could he read about that and eat pasta at the same time?* she wondered. He must be completely desensitised to the gore.

She was tired. It had been a long day of flying, concentrating and hiding. Andy broke into her thoughts.

'How is it going?' he thought to her.

'I've given up for the day. I'm coming home. I'll update you when I get there.'

She flew up through the bathroom fan, picked up her bag and flew out of the roof and back to base.

It was after ten when she arrived back at the house.

'Long day. Hungry?'

'Ravenous.'

'I got pizza.'

They both sat down to enjoy the food, and for a while all conversation ceased. The hot cheesy flan satiating like nothing else can.

'What'd you find out?'

Renee wiped tomato sauce from her mouth, 'where do I start?'

'Find the cop?'

'Eventually; I tried the warehouse first. Nothing. Then I went to the garage. There was a guy breaking into the place when I got there. There was a secret cupboard in the bathroom and the thief knew exactly where it was and how to get into it—it was hidden behind a false wall in the shower. He emptied it out—cash, jewellery and papers. Then he went to a pub and met Bill.'

'Bill? The drug runner we cleaned out?'

'Yep. He delivered all the stuff to him and Bill gave him an envelope—payment I assume. But the big thing was—Bill owns the garage. He knew all about the secret cupboard. The thief asked him if he was going to use the garage again and he said not for a while—it was too hot at the moment.'

'So he was their boss…'

'Yep. And for a moment there Andy, I very nearly took the ring off, I wanted to so badly. But then I thought—what if this guy isn't a crook—what if he is an undercover cop? We just don't know enough about him.'

'True,' Andy sighed. 'It's possible. I think we have to tell the police what we know and then let them work it out. Did you find anything out about the cop?'

'Yes. I was going to follow Bill, but I couldn't get out the door and he got away, and then I remembered my apartment, and I thought the policeman might be there, and anyway, I wanted to get some of my things—she said pointing at the satchel in the corner. 'He turned up while I was there.'

'Shit! Did he see you?'

'No, but unfortunately I had been rummaging around and he noticed that things were amiss. But I did manage to follow him back to his office—he works on the third floor of the headquarters in Surrey Hills. His name is Detective Inspector Tom Hayes—and I did a scan on is computer. He looks clean; he was even a whistle blower on an internal corruption case.'

'OK... how did you scan his computer? Actually, don't tell me, I don't want to know, it doesn't matter,' he had a piece of pizza half way to his mouth. 'The thing is, do you think we can trust him?'

'As far as I can tell—yes. I went back to his house and had a look around there as well, it all seems pretty normal. I don't know what else we can do. We are going to have to take a risk.'

'Yes. I think you're right. But still—under no circumstances do you show yourself to him. It could be the death of you if you do. Agreed?'

'Agreed.'

'Now we just have to work out how to make contact with him.'

Babayaga

The doctor climbed the basement stairs and carefully locked the door behind him. The door was concealed inside a large built-in cupboard in a store room, and once the door was closed it was almost impossible to see; you had to know where to look to find the lock. The cupboard had been built when the building was renovated many years ago. It was an old building, and the original plans failed to mention the basement, which was very convenient for their purposes. A two-way mirror on the cupboard door allowed him to exit the cupboard without being seen. He locked the door with the key hanging off the lanyard he wore around his neck. He let the key drop again and it made a clacking noise as it bounced against his security pass.

Such precautions were necessary. There were only a handful of people who knew of the existence of the basement, and more importantly, what was kept down there.

He flicked through the report again; the test results were good, very good. They had found a match. The client was willing to pay top dollar for two healthy kidneys. The breeder in question was getting too old for whelping and too ugly for prostitution. Besides, she was a pain in the arse and had a nasty habit of upsetting the others. Time to release some capital. He grinned at his own joke. She was costing them more than she was returning anyway. It was funny how they had actually been discussing whether they should terminate her last week, and now here was a lovely little money spinner to make it worthwhile. Bill would be pleased. He smiled to himself and started whistling as he exited the storeroom and walked into the hallway, shoes squeaking on the polished linoleum floor.

The boss had finally pissed off home. Bill walked down the corridor to the store room and let himself inside with the master key hanging on his lanyard. He unlocked the cupboard, climbing inside and closing the door behind him. He had a tiny LED torch on his key chain which gave him enough light to locate the keyhole. He closed the secret door behind him and walked down the narrow stairs to the basement. It was a real rabbit warren down here; dark tunnels stretching off in different directions. Most of it was unused and the old cement floors were covered in dust. He took the corridor leading to the right and walked towards an open door spilling light into the darkness.

The doctor was already there, sitting on an old leather couch. The room had a kitchenette along one wall and a coffee table and a couple of couches facing a TV at the other end. The room was lit by two florescent tubes and the furniture was old and sturdy but comfortable. The room was tidy, but had a grimy, dingy feel. It had not been vacuumed or wiped down in a long time.

'How did you manage to slip away?' Bill asked.

'He's given up watching me for the time being. You're his hobby now,' he said and smirked.

'The guy is a pervert.'

The doctor laughed loudly. 'Well I have some good news for you.'

'Oh, well that's a nice bloody change,' Bill said, grabbing a beer out of the fridge and throwing a second to the doctor.

The doctor caught it and placed it on the table to settle.

'The old whore—the liability—her kidneys are a perfect match for Mr. Hoegarth.'

'No shit! Excellent. Have you told Johnny yet?'

'Well, Johnny did ask me to terminate her and he isn't aware of Mr. Hoegarth's little problem, so I thought we might keep this between ourselves for once. Compensation for risk mitigation activities, as Johnny would say.'

It was Bill's turn to laugh, 'Sounds good to me. My neck is getting way too stretched. Can you write off the medical supplies without Johnny noticing?'

'Not a problem. I need certain things for a termination anyway, and everything else I've got in normal inventory. We'd have to run the furnace to get rid of her anyway, so that won't look odd. You should probably get rid of that other girl while we're at it, burn them both in the one go.'

'Yeah, you're probably right. Her rich daddy will realise she is missing at some point. He could make a pile of trouble. Pity, she would have been good for breeding.'

'And have the DNA trail do us in one day? No thanks. Better to use the drop outs and runaways that no one gives a shit about. And speaking of the DNA, you have got to stop messing with the breeding stock…'

'Oh come off it. The chances of anything being linked back to me are one in millions. It's not like I give my genetic profile away willy-nilly. These babies end up all over the world. Quit worrying. You should go and have some fun yourself.'

'No thanks. I prefer high end whores,' he said opening the beer at arm's length to avoid the spray. Beer slopped onto the floor.

'Johnny was asking about the slash and grab job the boys did. Do you have any idea what they thought they were doing?' Bill asked.

'None. What a fucking waste. We could have got 50 grand for that squealer, and the woman could have been reused too. It would have been a piece of piss to frame the hubby for her disappearance.'

'Yeah. Now he wants me to go and snare some more runaways to meet demand.'

'Bit risky given the current climate, isn't it? We still don't know what the hell happened to the boys; let alone who did it, or who knocked off your flat.'

'Yeah. But hey, it's not Johnny's problem, is it?' he said. 'Although, I am going to pay a visit to a nosey old bitch later tonight and see what she has to say about it all. She was poking around the garage after the boys got fried.'

'Did you manage to salvage anything from the garage?'

'Some cash and some paperwork; haven't been through it yet. Actually, I'd better do it now or Johnny will be harassing me again.'

'OK, I'm off to harvest some kidneys. I'll leave the furnace going all night if you need it,' the doctor said, taking his beer and heading down the hall.

'Ta,' Bill said, going to one of the cupboards and pulling out the cloth bag full of papers and cash. He grabbed himself another beer and went back to the couch.

He tipped the bag up, spilling the contents onto the coffee table. Papers and wads of cash slid over the surface.

He stacked the cash into piles, counting as he went.

'Sixty-four thousand,' he said and whistled. They owed him ten for the drug sales. So where had the other fifty come from? The car re-birthing might be ten or twenty, and as far as he knew, they hadn't shifted the kid, so what else had they been up to?

He turned to the paperwork.

There were details of the baby buyer who had pulled out of the sale. That might come in handy. Contacts for drug deals, he could pass that on to the new franchisee once he got it sorted.

He turned over another page and froze.

What the fuck? A photograph of a woman stared him in the face. Stapled to the back of it, in familiar handwriting was a note detailing her usual movements.

Those boys really were amateurs.

This was a definite keeper.

The Filigree Fork

Detective Inspector Hayes was reviewing CCTV footage from the areas around the warehouse when George tapped on the door.

'You gotta minute?'

'Sure. What's up?'

'We got some fingerprints from the break in at Rebecca Cole's place.'

'Any matches?'

'Yeah. Rebecca Cole.'

'Nothing in other words,' sighed Tom

'No. A big something. These are fresh prints.'

'What?!'

'There were two lots of prints on the boxes. Old prints covered with dust, and new prints on areas where the dust had been disturbed. Both sets of prints belonged to Rebecca Cole.'

'So she's not dead.'

'Well someone could have made up some fake prints and planted them.'

'Pretty unlikely I would think.'

'That's not my call—I deal in the facts.'

'Thanks George. Did you find anything else?'

'Nothing so far.'

'Well, you have given me some more food for thought. Thanks mate.'

'No problemo. I'm doing a coffee run—want one?'

'Nah, I've had too many today already.'

He left Tom to mull over the latest developments.

So, she was still alive somewhere. That was incredible to say the least; especially after what he had found this morning. One of the CCTV cameras down by the docks had captured an image of the warehouse. The camera was focused on a much closer building, but in the background it showed two men breaking into the warehouse's side door. Half an hour later a car had pulled up—he was certain it was the one that had been later found burnt out. A bald man had emerged and dragged a woman inside.

Later again, the three men left the building and piled into the car; one of them carrying something small wrapped in cloth. He would bet his life it was the three men who had been fried at the garage.

Not long after the car had left an old man had gone into the warehouse. Moments later he had emerged again and had run as fast as his old legs could carry him.

So, there was a witness; an old man. He would bet that it was the same old guy that had been hanging around the next day. If only they had spoken to him at the scene on day one. He would not be easy to find; he obviously didn't want to talk to police.

He zoomed in on the old man and printed off a copy of the screen. Maybe one of the beat cops would know who he was. Gardiner and Peale seemed pretty cluey; he'd ask them to keep an eye out too.

He had fast-forwarded through the remaining CCTV footage, and had found the arrival of the real estate agent who had called the job in and the arrival of the police. Rebecca Cole did not leave through the side door in that time. He reviewed the crime scene notes again. No other sign of forced entry. Where had the body gone and how? There must be another way into the building.

He grabbed his jacket and headed down the stairs. George was on his way up with a tray of coffees.

'Have you got an hour to spare to do some fingerprint work for me?'

'Now?'

'Yeah. I'm heading back to the warehouse.'

'Give me five, and I'll drop these off and grab my stuff.'

'Okay—meet me in the garage.'

Tom walked down to his car and leaned on the side of it.

She must have got out of the building another way. But where would she go? The blood loss would have been critical; surely she couldn't have made it out alone. Maybe the old man came back to help her? In and out via another way?

But she hadn't gone to any of the local hospitals, they had checked them all. So who looked after her, and how was she well enough to go rummaging through her apartment a week or so after that? Was she faking her death? Why did she want to disappear? Or did someone else want her to disappear? Or was there something deeper to all this—were the fingerprints fake after all?

What was going on?

Tom was still deep in thought when George arrived at the car with coffee in hand.

'Ready?' George asked him, startling him out of his thoughts.

'Oh, yeah. Sorry. I was off with the fairies.'

At the warehouse they checked every wall for loose tin or planks. There was no way to access the roof. It would be impossible for someone to enter the building without going past the CCTV cameras out the front. They walked back to the car.

'This one is under your skin isn't it?' George asked Tom.

'Yep; either I'll solve it or I'll go mad trying.'

They drove back to the office.

They had worked out their plan to lure Detective Inspector Hayes to the local pub for a chat, and had just finished going through their emergency escape plan, when there was a knock at the door.

Renee shrank and flew onto the top of a kitchen cupboard as Andy made his way to the front door.

A moment later and he reappeared with Bruce trailing behind him.

'Cuppa?'

'Yeah, ta.'

Renee reappeared. 'Hi Bruce. You look frazzled.'

'It's been a shitty morning,' he said, pulling out a kitchen chair and lowering himself into it.

'What's up?' Andy asked passing out cups of tea, and taking a seat.

'I went down to see old Babayaga—she lives in a park down near The Rocks,' he explained to Renee, 'She sees and hears everything. She takes a lot of the runaways under her wing—warns them of places to stay clear of, and shows them where they can get a feed and a safe bed,' he stopped, cleared his throat, and looked at the ceiling.

'No...' said Andy.

'Last night,' Bruce said with a nod.

Renee was at a loss. The two old friends were speaking a silent language she couldn't follow.

'Has something happened to her?'

'Yeah,' said Bruce, and she waited for him to compose himself. 'One of the girls found her this morning. Someone tortured her, and then they killed her.'

'Do the girls know who did it?' she asked.

'The Stonefish. Babayaga warned them about him. One of the others said he was also known as "Bill".'

'Bill? Is this the same Bill that had me killed? But why would he kill her? Torture her?' she said.

'She's been a thorn in his side for years, but he just found out that she witnessed the death of the mechanics. Apparently, he wanted to know everything.'

'Did she see everything?'

'I don't know.'

'So this monster, this Stonefish, Bill, might know that I exist?'

'Possibly. Whether he believed her or not, who knows?'

'He killed her because of me...'

'No—he killed her because he is a murdering arsehole. You are just as much his victim as Babayaga is. You did not cause this,' said Bruce.

'We robbed him Andy!'

'He doesn't know that.'

'What if she told him about me, about a fairy, and he has put two and two together?'

'That is a very long shot,' said Bruce.

'It doesn't matter what he does or doesn't know. We all know what he did to you and to Babayaga—and that is unforgivable,' said Andy, looking from one to the other. 'We have to stop him. We have to tell the police everything we know about Bill, the baby racket and Babayaga. Agreed?'

'Yep.'

'Yes!'

Bill slipped into the cupboard and down the stairs with the carry-all.

What a pointless fucken waste of time last night had been; stupid old drunk hallucinating about fairies.

Well at least she wouldn't be helping any more runaways.

He threw the bag full of bloody clothes into the furnace; thankfully, it was still burning from the night before. He would come down later tonight and stir through the ashes; make sure everything was completely burned.

Last night he had gone to see what she knew, fully expecting to scare the information out of her and shut her up for good. Instead, she had ruffled him. Nobody ever did that to him.

When he got up close to her, he had the strange feeling that he knew her. But that had been twenty years ago—*she* couldn't still be alive…

…but it was the exact same place.

He lifted his shirt sleeve and looked at the wizened brown scar on his wrist. It was a burn; a filigree pattern of raised skin.

Twenty years ago, the woman had lifted his sleeve and told him 'You have sealed your own fate. The end is nigh. The door will open soon!'

Babayaga did the same thing last night and said the exact same words.

For a moment he had freaked out. 'I should have killed you twenty years ago!' He had shouted at her grabbing her by the throat.

Then he had taken his time; keeping her alive as long as possible.

It hadn't helped.

He still felt the sick dread.

A Policeman and a Pub

The next day Detective Inspector Hayes checked all the hospitals again. Then he went and made a call to all the dodgy backyard doctors in the area; still nothing.

He checked all the CCTV camera footage from around Rebecca's flat. There were a couple of cameras around the area, and it would have been almost impossible for her to avoid them all. But they showed nothing. How did she get in without being seen and what had she been looking for?

Then there was Babayaga. He sighed.

She had been a figure on the edge of his consciousness for most of his life. See seemed ageless. She had always been there, helping the runaways and strays. He had offered her money one time and she had immediately passed it on to one of her waifs. She needed no one.

Until now...

No one had been there for her.

Whoever had killed her had taken his time; gutting her with patience and precision and with absolutely no fear of discovery.

It was getting late; the sun was starting to set. It had been a completely wasted day. He walked down to the car park and was just about to open his car door when a glowing green light whizzed past his eyes and came to a halt a few feet away. It had given him quite a fright, and now he was in a state of astonishment, wondering what on earth it was and whether it was as dangerous as the scene at the garage would suggest. He cautiously inched toward it trying to get a better look. The glow was too bright to see what was making it.

As he took another step forward the light moved a few feet away from him. It was the Christmas beetle again, he was sure of it. He stood watching it for a while and then decided to try and get a photo of it. He had a smart phone in the glove box of his car.

As soon as he turned towards the car the light flew back at him and circled his head. He ducked, expecting it to bite him. As soon as he stopped moving the light came to a standstill and hovered in front of him again. He approached it again, and again it moved slowly away from him, but this time it continued slowly in the direction of the exit. He followed it a little way and then stopped. The light stopped again and started to move back towards him. As soon as he started to approach it again it resumed its journey to the exit.

Okay, it obviously wanted him to follow it. His curiosity had got the better of him; he followed.

It led him towards the old industrial district, never getting too far ahead of him, always stopping or circling back if he hesitated. He followed it down a dark lane bordered by run down terrace houses with untidy yards and peeling paint. Finally, the light turned onto a larger street, Baker Street. There was an old pub built into the corner of an old two story building and the light bobbed towards it. The Contented Soul.

An old man was standing leaning against the outside wall of the pub smoking.

'Nice evening for a stroll,' he said casually.

'You could say that,' Tom replied mystified.

The light paused near the old man's ear for a moment and then zipped away over the building and disappeared into the darkness. For a moment, Tom thought he had seen a tiny figure inside the light.

'What was that?' he asked the old man, glancing towards the roof.

'Oh I wouldn't be too concerned about that if I was you,' he said.

The policeman frowned.

'Do you believe in ghosties and ghoulies and long legged beasties?' asked Andy.

'No.'

'Well it's time you started.'

'But what is it?'

'Can't rightly say. I help it; it helps me, better just to leave it at that. But I do think that you should come in and have a beer.'

He took the bait and followed the old man into the pub. He was sure it was the man who had evaded them at the warehouse.

The pub was busy.

'Bob,' the old man greeted the bartender.

'What'll it be, Andy?'

'Guinness?' He asked turning to the policeman. Tom nodded, 'Two pints of Guinness please, Bob.'

Bob started the glasses and then raced off to fill other orders while the thick, dark ale settled.

They waited in silence until Bob returned to top up their glasses, and then Andy led him to a table near the window.

They settled into their seats and Andy looked around. There was no one close enough to overhear. He looked at the policemen.

'First things first; I know some stuff. You know that I know some stuff, but if you try to get me into any witness box I will act like a crazy old drunk and there are plenty around here that will testify that that is what I am. Understood?'

'Completely,' Tom answered lifting his beer and taking sip.

'Fine. We know where we stand.' He took a large pull on his beer, downing half in one go.

'Now… Detective Inspector Hayes, I know you are looking into what happened at the warehouse. I also know that you are working on the three bastards that got fried at the garage. The two incidents are related—I dare say you suspect that already.'

The policeman was surprised, but tried not to show it. He decided to let the old man talk.

'The woman at the warehouse, Rebecca, was killed by that bunch of shit. They cut her baby out of her and left her to bleed to death on the floor. They had a buyer for the baby. They were dealers. Drugs and babies. But this is the first time they've murdered for one as far as I know.' He took a sip of his beer. 'They were pimps as well—so usually it is the unwanted kids from their harem that they sell.'

'How do you know all this?'

'I know people who know—I'm not going to give you sources. But I can give you some background and maybe even tell you where you might find some answers.'

'I'll take any information you can give me. The whole thing reeks.'

'For starters, don't bother trying to find Rebecca's body. It is gone for good. Don't bother trying to find the baby—it is dead and buried— somewhere you will never find it.

'The three that got burned at the garage were the ones who actually did the deed, but they are small fish. There are bigger, nastier fish above them—those are the ones you want to fry.' He took another sip of his beer and looked the policeman in the eye.

'Go and ask the local prostitutes what they know about the Stonefish.'

'I've never heard of the Stonefish,' Tom said.

'I'd be surprised if you had. He's like a myth around here. They call him that because he hides in amongst them—camouflaged—devouring all that he can, and if you get too close he pumps a pint of poison into you. He's a bogey man. Half the people you talk to will tell you they have never heard of him. Others will tell you straight up that he doesn't exist and the rest will refuse to talk to you at all.

'Keep your eyes on the young runaways that turn up around the docks. Before too long, he'll send someone out to have a chat with them. Or he'll just take them,' Andy said. The detective noticed that Andy was watching him closely, trying to gauge his reactions.

'Rumour has it that he has an underground den where he provides underage girls (and boys) for big bucks. He uses some of them to breed babies for his baby racket. Apparently, he is also a sadistic S.O.B. Hardly surprising considering.

'I can't tell you his name or what he looks like or where he lives, but I know someone who can.'

'I'm listening.'

'They call him Bill around here. Some people think he is the Stonefish— I don't know if that's true or not. One way or the other, Bill is a complete bastard.' Andy passed a sheet of paper across the table to Tom. It was a hand-drawn map.

'That's the address of the flat he has been using lately, he likes to use secret cupboards to stash things in. You might want to take a look behind the shower at the garage, although I think that one has been cleaned out now. And that,' he said pointing to another point on the map, 'is where he has been seen passing supplies to his drug couriers. He sits on one of the benches. He uses a laptop bag to deliver to his boys. One of his drug couriers works from that café,' he said pointing to yet another mark on the map. 'And he often hangs out at that pub,' he said pointing to "The Rose and Crown."

Then he passed two photos across the table; Bill and the thief.

'I know that Bill was involved in the murder at the warehouse, and I know that he was the drug supplier for the three dealers that got incinerated. I also know that he has abducted at least one street kid, possibly more. Some of the independent prostitutes arrange their business very carefully so that they never have to run into him. This other guy is one of his henchmen.'

'How did the three dealers die?'

'I don't know,' he said looking him straight in the eyes. 'I've never heard of anything like that before.'

'No. Neither have I. Weird shit seems to be the order of the day at the moment.' He sighed and sipped his beer.

'He also killed Babayaga two days ago.'

Tom looked at him intently. 'Is that why you decided to talk to me?'

'Partly... Did you know she could speak English?'

'No.'

'Neither did he—until recently.'

'Is that why he killed her?'

'I guess so. She knew too much. And she knew how to hide the runaways from him. He didn't like that.'

He sat in silence for a moment, watching the policeman.

'That's all I have for you at the moment, but I daresay you can make something out of it.'

Tom finished his beer. 'I don't suppose you want me dropping around here looking for you too often.'

'Nope.'

'Here, this is my mobile,' he said passing Andy a business card. 'If I need to get in touch, how can I reach you?'

'Here.' Andy passed him a piece of paper with a mobile phone number on it. 'It's on silent a lot of the time, so don't be surprised if I take a while to get back to you.'

'Why are you putting your neck on the line like this?' he asked Andy.

'I'm old—I've seen some horrors in my time, but this... No. It has to stop somewhere. If they get me, they get me. I've lived a long life. Not that I am going to let them get me. If you roast me on this—I will know—and I will disappear so quick that you'll think I was a ghost.'

'Don't worry. None of your details will appear in anything. I don't even know your name.'

'No, you don't. But I daresay you will soon enough. And someone in the force will be looking over your shoulder, wondering why you accessed my records, so make sure you have a good excuse when they come knocking. I dare say the Stonefish has some friends in the police force somewhere.'

'So how do you know you can trust me?'

'I've made enquiries. I can't be sure, but you seem okay. Time will tell.'

'Well... thanks. This could make a big difference. I'll be in touch,' he said, rising from his seat. He walked out of the pub and walked off into the night.

Andy sat back down in his seat and finished his beer. Renee appeared from behind a poster on the wall and slipped into his pocket.

'What do you think?' she asked once she had established a link.

'Not sure. I think you need to follow him and see what he does next. He knows the green light he has been seeing is connected to me now. You cannot be seen. You cannot be seen at all. Okay? Be careful of mirrors and reflective surfaces—anywhere he might catch a glimpse of you. Let me know what he finds.'

She turned into a beetle. He got up and went outside, making sure she had time to slip through the door. She flew after the policeman. Andy leaned against the wall and lit another cigarette, pondering their next move.

It was completely dark by the time he walked back through the suburb to his car in the police garage. He unlocked his car and thought about driving home, but changed his mind. Instead, he locked the car and went back upstairs into the building. He swiped his pass at the door and caught the elevator to the third floor. The corridor that led to his office was carpeted, muffling his footsteps; only a few offices here and there had their lights on. It was very quiet. He walked into his office and shut the door behind him.

As he sat down, a small insect the size of a flea flew off his hair and landed on a coat hanging on the coat rack behind him.

She made herself a tiny bit bigger to make it easier to see what was going on, but made sure that her glow was off.

There was a grainy computer print draped on his keyboard. It looked like a still from a security camera. It was a picture of Andy. Written across the bottom was a note:

Tom, this looks like an old bloke who lives near the docks. He hangs out at 'The Contented Soul' —a pub in Baker Street. His name is Andy Roswald. Hope it helps,
    cheers Doug.

The detective picked it up and smiled.

'You little beauty, Doug; I owe you a beer or three.'

He logged onto his computer and within a minute was doing a search on Andy Roswald. It came back with an immigration record, an Australian citizenship record and a few links to rates notices and utility companies.

Tom leaned back in his chair, his hands behind his head like a pillow.

'No drivers licence, no pension, no social security records at all. No bank account. This guy is almost off the grid.' Tom said to himself.

She had sat listening to him talking to Andy in the pub, and had decided he was an intelligent, thoughtful man. He seemed a gentle giant, and wondered what he would be like in a violent situation. Although he had the build to be able to handle himself, she found it hard to imagine him throwing a punch at someone.

She looked at his face and decided he was actually quite handsome, although she hadn't noticed it at first. He had wonderful bright blue eyes. Even from here she could smell his subtle scent.

She saw him type in a search for 'stonefish'. He got one vague reference to an unidentified underworld criminal. No other aliases, no known hangouts and no other references.

He picked up the phone and dialled a number.

'You got a minute Peter? Got some photos I'd like you to have a look at. I'd rather this was just between you and me at the moment.'

She heard could hear a garbled response, but it was not clear enough for her to interpret what was said.

'OK. I'll be there in five,' he said

She shrank herself quickly and flew into the breast pocket of his jacket, bumping against the inside of the pocket as he picked it up and slid it on.

They travelled down in the lift and got out on the second floor. Tom walked over to an office and knocked on the door. The sign on the front said "Detective Inspector Peter Symonds".

'Come in.'

He opened the door and stepped inside.

'What have you got for me?'

Tom closed the door behind him. Inside his pocket she wriggled a little higher so she could get a view of the new comer.

'Ever seen this guy before?' Tom asked as he passed the photos of Bill across the desk and sat down in the spare chair.

'Yeah, I have actually. Bill Doyle. He works at a posh nursing home over in Double Bay. We had some trouble on the waterfront a few months back and he gave us a tip off about some dealing he saw going on in the area.'

'Is he into anything shady?'

'Not that I am aware of.'

'You might want to see if you can find any connection between him and the three mechanics that got fried.'

'Really?' Peter said surprised. 'Can you reveal your source?'

'Not at the moment, but I am starting to think that we may be working together on this.'

'You think he's linked to the Cole murder?'

'Looks like it. Ever heard of "The Stonefish?"'

'Yeah, but the jury is out on whether it is an urban myth or not.'

'My source says Bill here,' pointing at the photo, 'is either the Stonefish's right hand man, or even the Stonefish himself.'

Peter raised his eyebrows.

'Does your source have a death wish? Because, if this is true, they could easily end up in a body bag.'

'The source is aware of the risks. Sounds like Babayaga has already paid the price.'

'Bloody hell,' he said quietly. 'I heard about that. OK. If half the rumours about the Stonefish are true, this could be a huge win for us. Tell me everything.'

Tom gave him a rundown of what Andy had told him about Bill and the Stonefish and showed him the map.

'My source thought it was likely that the Stonefish had an insider in the force. I've known you long enough to know it isn't you, so for the time being, I would like to keep this between ourselves.'

'I think that's wise. That means no organised physical surveillance yet, but I can do some record checks on Bill. And maybe some unofficial surveillance when I am in the area.'

'Okay, I'll see what I can dig up as well and let you know,' said Tom.

'Agreed. I'll keep you in the loop. Oh and by the way, have forensics come up with anything from the incineration?'

'Nope. And I won't be holding my breath.'

'Yeah. Good luck with that one,' Peter chuckled as Tom left the office.

Renee pulled her head back down into his pocket.

It had been a long day and she was feeling drowsy. His pocket was warm and soft and her claws were hooked into the fabric so she didn't even have to exert herself hold herself up. It was a comforting feeling. She felt like an injured animal, tucked away in a warm, dark, quiet place.

Would she ever heal?

A Close Encounter

She awoke, unaware that she had fallen asleep and unsure of where she was. Her beetle claws were entangled in the threads of something. It was a moment before she remembered that she was in Tom's coat pocket. She turned back to her usual (small) self and untangled her arms, dropping into the dark depths of the pocket. It was dark and dusty at the bottom, lint and loose threads cushioning her fall. The coat wasn't warm anymore, and she couldn't smell him. He must have taken it off. She carefully flitted to the top of the pocket and peeked out. It was hanging on a hook on the wall next to an umbrella. She was in his house again.

She flew up onto a shelf above the coat rack and turned back into a beetle. There was a light on in the lounge room and she flew over and landed on the light shade. Tom was sitting on the couch, a laptop balanced on his knees and several papers spread around him on the couch and the floor. There was an empty dinner plate resting on the coffee table and the smell of cooling food wafting from the kitchen; some kind of stir-fry. She wondered if there was any left, suddenly aware of her empty stomach.

She must have been sleeping for some time. The clock in the kitchen showed it was after 1 AM.

Didn't he ever sleep?

Something was bugging him. He was flicking from one report to another and back again. He sighed and leaned back, rubbing his eyes. She took the opportunity to land on the back of the couch. It was all about her; forensics, photos, financial statements, witness accounts—all of it—disjointed fragments of her life.

She felt incredibly humbled and devastated at the same time. That this man should be devoting so much of his own time to finding her

124

killers was both a light in the darkness and an incredible tragedy. Why was he frittering his life away chasing a ghost?

His head had lolled against the back of the couch and he was breathing deeply; asleep. The laptop was threatening to slide off his lap. She flew to the centre of the room and returned to full size, leaning over to gently push the laptop onto the couch beside him before it could fall to the floor. The edge of her wing gently brushed his face as she stood up and he awoke with a start.

She was gone before he could properly register her presence; before he was fully awake. For a millisecond he had seen Rebecca's startled face close to his own. Her eyes had been like an explosion of fireworks; like vivid green opals. Like the green hue of a Christmas beetle. He shook himself out of his incredibly weird, vivid dream and took himself off to bed.

Renee watched him leave the room and breathed a sigh of relief. She heard a door close further up the hallway and returned to full size to get a better look at the papers strewn on and around the table. A picture—the body of an old woman; horribly disfigured. Babayaga…

Seeing this, she understood completely that she was not a monster; Bill was. She suddenly wished she had burnt him to ashes when she had the chance. If she had, Babayaga would still be alive. How many more people were going to die before he was brought to justice? It was all too slow!

A sudden movement caught her eye and she turned to see Tom re-enter the room; barefoot, wet hair, naked except for a towel around his waist. He had not made a sound. He was not looking in her direction—he had not seen her yet. In an instant she was a beetle, fumbling on the table. She tried to turn so she could see where he was, but suddenly she was engulfed in darkness.

'How the hell did you get in here you silly bugger,' he said, lifting a hand just enough to peer in at the beetle trapped in his hands.

Oh no! He's going to kill me! I have to get away. She started to buzz in panic, trying to escape through the gap in his fingers.

'Settle petal,' he said in a soothing voice, closing his hands again to stop the beetle escaping. 'I'm not going to hurt you.'

He walked over to the back door, nudging the door handle with his elbow to open it, and gently tipped the beetle into a potted tomato bush on the back veranda. He looked at it carefully. It was a typical Christmas Beetle; pale brown with pink and green opalescent highlights; nothing unusual about it. So why did he feel like he was being stalked by beetles at the moment?

His towel began to slip and he quickly righted it and hurried back inside; suddenly conscious of the fact he was outside and half naked.

Renee collapsed in the pot until her breathing returned to normal. She wasn't entirely sure that it was the danger of the situation that had made her breathless.

Andy was already in bed when she returned. She would have liked to have spoken to him about what she has seen and heard, but did not want to wake him.

She trusted Tom. It was funny; it was like it had been with Andy, a kind of sixth sense. It was a feeling of being able to depend on him; but without really knowing why. He was obviously a dedicated policeman, but that by itself was not enough to promote such a trust, and although she admitted to herself that she found him attractive, she was not blinded by a deep affection for him. In any case, she was ready to pass on anything that she could find to him.

There was nothing that she could do to turn back time, to bring her baby James back from the dead or bring her old life back, but at least she might stop these killers from torturing any other kids, any more old women.

Once they were stopped, she might even be able to do some good for the world somehow.

She wished that she had been able to get hold of the papers from the garage. Bill had them now. She wondered if he was still using the lair that they had raided, whether they would be in his safe. But it was unlikely. He had been burnt once; he would be stupid to trust that hiding place a second time.

She might be able to find him at the café or the park. Maybe tomorrow.

She wanted this to be over now.

Tom

Over breakfast she updated Andy on her discoveries.

'You were right, Tom knows your name. As soon as he got back to the office he did a search on you. He knows you live here.'

'I would have thought less of him if he hadn't. For all he knows I am a complete nutter. Better to get a bit of an idea of who you are dealing with. Did he seem to take it seriously?'

'Extremely; to the point where he went and spoke to an officer from the drugs squad. A man named Peter. Tom obviously trusts him completely. He warned him that there might be a mole in the force and they agreed to keep everything low key and not involve any one else for the moment. Peter was very interested in the Stonefish; sounds like he has been after him for a long time.'

'Good. We've got the ball rolling at least.' He leaned back in his chair and looked at her. She was coping extremely well all things considered. It probably helped a lot having a wondrous set of new talents to explore and a vendetta to concentrate on. He also noticed that she was thinking of the cop as "Tom" now.

'I was thinking,' she said, breaking into his thoughts, 'the papers that I saw taken from the safe in the garage—Bill has them now. They might be worth having.'

'Yes. Very. But the problem is, if we go and steal them, even if they contain information that will damn him to Hell, it won't be any good as evidence. We need to find them and then let Detective Hayes know where they are. That way he can get a proper warrant.'

'What if Bill destroys them?'

'He might have already. How are we to know? We could get photos of them though. Still wouldn't be any good as evidence, but the cops would at least have the information.'

'Do you think he would have hidden them at the flat we raided?'

'I doubt it. He won't think it is safe anymore. Still, it's worth a look, I suppose. Otherwise if we keep an eye on Bill, he might lead us to them.'

Tom went down the stairs to the Crime Scene Section; they were tucked away in the basement. He knocked on the door of George's office.

'Come in,' George bellowed from inside.

Tom usually avoided this place, the smell of formaldehyde made him feel ill.

'Waazup,' George said, eyeing him as he scrapped dirt off a plaster cast of a shoe print.

'Have you guys finished processing the items from the garage crime scene?'

'Home of the incredible powdered mechanics? Most of it; what do you need?' he said putting down the cast and moving towards a row of evidence lockers.

'There was a laptop at the scene, has that been analysed yet?'

'Partly,' George said, changing direction and moving over to a desk covered in computer gear. 'Dennis cracked the password and has done a full drive backup and software list, and he's started to recover the deleted files. He hasn't had a chance to go through the contents yet. There was one thing that may be of interest though—let me grab the report.' He logged onto a terminal and searched through the file structure, finally opening a document.

'Here it is.' He scrolled to a section labelled "Preliminary Findings".

'The laptop had a program called "Second Copy" installed—file backup software,' he said glancing at Tom. 'The interesting thing is that it had a regular backup scheduled for a folder in the temp drive.'

'So?'

'The profile name was called "backup to USB" and it was set to copy this temp folder to a USB stick and then automatically delete the contents of the folder off the laptop.'

'Was there a USB stick in amongst the stuff at the garage?'

'Nope.'

'What are the chances that Dennis will be able to recover those deleted files?'

'Hard to say; they've been copying and deleting to that folder pretty regularly; depends how segmented the drive is. You won't be getting it any time soon anyway.'

'How much longer have we got on the warrant for the garage?'

'Another week; then it goes back to the owner.'

'Who is the owner anyway?'

'It's a company. I haven't got the full details yet, but it's called... hang on a minute, it's here somewhere, he said scrolling back up the document to the first page, 'Sydney Logistics, Utilities and Transportation Solutions'.

'Let me see that,' said Tom coming over to read over his shoulder. 'Oh these guys are a real class act! How did they get that one past the Australian Business Register?'

'Wha...?'

'Initials.'

'Oh...'

'I'd better go over and have another look at the garage. Are you up for a little excursion? I have a tip off I want to follow up.'

'Sure. I'm sick to death of plaster casts at the moment. All this dust makes me sneeze.'

Renee was back at Bill's flat. The place was deserted. All the furniture was gone and the hidden cupboard had been removed. It was just a normal wardrobe again. At first, she doubted herself; thought she had gone to the wrong place, but then she recognised a scratch on the kitchen floor and a burn mark on the kitchen bench. Had Bill packed up and moved on somewhere else? It made sense. His nest had been robbed—time to start again.

She wondered if she would find him in the park.

Bill wasn't there, but Peter-the-drug-squad-cop was. He was sitting to one side of Bill's usual haunt eating a hamburger. He was eating it extremely slowly. She wondered how long he could stretch it out.

Twenty minutes later he gave up, and so did she. She followed Peter to the drug dealer's café. Bill wasn't there either.

She left Peter ordering more food at the café and headed to the pub.

The pub was very busy, but Bill wasn't there either. Where was he?

At work... Where did the policeman say that he worked? It was a hospice or something; near the water; a posh one. She flew down towards the harbour.

Bill was running a big risk. He had only been able to restock his boys in the evening after work, so he had been giving them more stock than he was comfortable with. More stock meant bigger losses if they got done over or arrested, and bigger gaol terms. It also meant a higher risk of the runner ingesting some of the product; for some stupid reason, they thought it was less likely to be noticed.

His boss was being obsessive about his attendance and regularly noting his whereabouts. It was seriously curtailing his business. A half hour lunch break was not long enough to stock up and pass on. He needed Johnny to use his influence to get him off his case.

Time seemed to stand still as he worked, constantly checking the clock, and waiting for his break. He was out the door the second the clock ticked over and walked to a quiet section of the local park to call Johnny.

'It's me. You have got to get this jackass off my back. I can't get the boys restocked during the day; I have to give them double rations at night. We are gunna get ripped off again.'

'And yet in spite of that, the only place that gets ripped off is your place...'

'What is that supposed to mean?'

'Never mind, Billy boy,' he sighed. 'I will speak to the administrator right now. Tomorrow it will be business as usual.'

'Good.'

'Happy now?'

The phone clicked, and then hummed in his ear. He turned it off and jammed it back into his pocket.

'Fuck wit.'

They slipped under the police tape and Tom unlocked the front door.

George had his camera slung around his neck and a forensic tool box in his hand. They pushed open the door and paused just inside the threshold. The three greasy burn marks on the floor were sobering.

'Any ideas yet?' Tom asked him.

'Nothing sensible.'

Tom nodded and passed to one side of the markings, reluctant to walk over them.

'In the bathroom,' he said to George, and moved to the far side of the garage.

The room smelled of urine and mildew; the ceiling freckled with black spots.

Tom froze.

'Your guys haven't been back in here have they?'

'No.'

'Those tyres and tins were in the shower the last time I was here.'

'Yes. They were.'

'This is getting to be a recurring theme, isn't it?'

'Let me check for prints. Maybe Rebecca's ghost has been hanging out here too.'

'Check the shower—I was told there is a cupboard or something behind it.' Opposite the shower was a change area with a wooden bench and Tom sat down to survey the bathroom while George tried to lift some prints.

The back of the shower was made of grubby sheets of waterproof panelling, thin strips of plastic joining them together. George concentrated his efforts on the areas around the joins.

'No good,' he said. 'There are smudges in the grime here and here,' he said pointing at the panels. 'No prints—looks like they were wearing gloves.'

Tom got up and ran his hands along the edges, trying to get his fingers under the join. 'This side here, the join isn't right,' Tom said.

George slipped a flat bladed knife out of his toolbox and slid it under the join. 'Yeah. It's really loose. I can probably get a crow bar under it, but it will do some damage.'

'Go for it.'

George retrieved a crow bar from the tool rack on the garage wall.

He tore the edge of the panel to pieces trying to get decent leverage, but eventually the lock gave way and the panel swivelled open.

The large floor safe inside was already open. And empty.

'What a surprise,' said Tom, 'I suspect there won't be any fingerprints either,' he said. George began to dust the area around the dial on the safe.

'Nope,' he said standing up again, 'it's a complete waste of time.'

'Actually—no—it's not. It turns out my source is spot on,' said Tom.

'I see... Actually—I don't... But I don't give a shit either. Anything else you want done while we're here?'

Tom laughed, 'I don't suppose your lot made any progress on the names of the other two mechanics?'

'Yes. We did. You want names and addresses?'

'Sure.'

'Walk this way,' he said walking out of the building and locking up after them.

He pulled a laptop from the car, and booted it up.

'Here you go,' he said turning the screen to face the policeman.

Tom used his smart phone to take a photo of the document and made sure the names and addresses were clear.

'OK. We're done here. Have any of your guys been to visit these addresses yet?'

'Yep. All taped off and processed. They were both loners. I have keys back at the lab for the second place, but the first guy, Jeff Layton, lived in a serviced apartment. It looks like he was the brains of the operation. The concierge will be able to let you in.'

Tom looked around the foyer, taking in the marble floors and polished brass while he waited. This was high class accommodation.

The concierge was thorough and efficient. The initial search had been unsettling and he had been sure to obtain a police contact should anything else arise. He mentally patted himself on the back, marvelling at his own good sense, as he called them now. The name, service number and general physical description of the policeman in front of him matched. He sighed with relief. The last thing he wanted was more scandal. He hung up and retrieved the keys to the apartment.

Tom noticed the change in demeanour instantly. All suspicion had evaporated, replaced with relieved face, eager to be of assistance. He was guided to the elevators and escorted to the fifth floor.

They stepped from the elevator into a hall with thick luxurious carpet. The door was obvious; police tape crossing its surface. A frown crossed the brow of his companion.

'I don't suppose we can remove that now?'

'Afraid not; a forensic member will come and remove it once we're finished.'

The concierge nodded reluctantly and unlocked the door for him.

'Must get back to business,' he said and retreated to the elevators.

Tom got the distinct impression that he didn't want to be seen anywhere near the offending tape.

The apartment was sparsely furnished; white carpet, black leather chair, kitchen to one side with an excess of stainless steel appliances. A door to the right opened into a study, a bedroom through the door on the left.

Traces of fingerprinting talc stood out on the dining table and black marble kitchen benches, ruining the otherwise immaculate presentation. No dirty dishes, no discarded clothes.

He did a quick search of all the usual hiding places, but did not expect to find anything. He left the study to last. Mr. clean and efficient would probably want all his paperwork to hand.

Where would he hide a USB stick? There were plenty of nooks and crannies in the elaborate desk, but he couldn't find any hidden panels or drawers. All the power points and light fittings were legit. That was too easy anyway; these guys liked to push it.

There was a bookcase built in to one of the walls. He pulled each of the books out one at a time, flicking through them for cavities. He checked inside vases and containers and checked under a statue to see if there was a false bottom. Nothing.

The desk was in disarray; the forensic team had disconnected the computer and taken it away for analysis. He would have to ask them later if they had discovered anything hidden in the PC box. They had left the monitor on the desk; disconnected cables hanging out of the back of it like entrails. He ran his hands over and around the monitor, looking for any loose plastic, and then looked at the back of it. There was a plastic panel covering the connections for the power cable and computer cable, to make it look neater no doubt. He lifted it off. In the cavity behind it, stuck to the back of the monitor with a piece of putty was a USB stick. Bingo. He was a little disappointed, and surprised that the forensics team had missed it. It seemed a bit too easy. Did he keep it simple so he could access it quickly, or was this a red herring? He wondered if the stick would be blank.

He called George to come and collect it.

Clio

Renee was frustrated. She had been unable to locate Bill's workplace; there were too many nursing homes in the area.

'Let's go out and get a coffee. I want to feel human for a while,' she said to Andy, 'then we can go and watch the park for a while and see if Bill turns up.'

'Yep. Sounds like a plan.' He grabbed his coat and locked the front door behind them. He wasn't conscious of it, but he was enjoying himself immensely. The past few days had a distinctly Nancy flavour about them. He had missed their intrigues and adventures.

They had only just turned a corner onto the main street when they suddenly felt an incredible power surging around them. Wherever they were, they were close.

'Oh my God, there are hundreds of them!' Andy breathed.

She didn't have to ask what he meant; she could feel them too, all around them.

'What do they want?' she asked him.

'I don't know. But they can't do anything to us here; too many people about.'

He guided her over to one of the cafes and he chose an outside table where there were plenty of people walking past.

A waiter came over and took their order; once he had left Andy opened up a thought stream with her.

They are just watching us at the moment, but they must have some kind of a plan. There are too many of them for this to be anything but an ambush. Maybe they thought we would run again? he said.

What are we going to do? We can't stay here forever. They can't sense you can they?—it's me they are homing in on. Is there any way I can shield myself from them?' she asked.

'Nancy knew the spell, but I don't I'm afraid.'

Their coffees arrived and they sat sipping them slowly, the standoff continuing. Renee tried to work out how many there were and where they were hiding. She could sense at least three of them up in the awning of the café, and she spotted a dull glow in the supports of the umbrella spread over the table next to them.

Suddenly a tall, elegant woman with long brown hair walked over to their table, pulled out a chair out and sat down. It was the same woman from the memory that Andy had shown her, but simply dressed; wings hidden.

'Shit—it's Queen Clio.'

'Well aren't you going to say "hello"?' she said languidly, leaning back in her chair. She was wearing a black knee-length skirt and a white blouse with a brown leather jacket. The collar of the shirt had a pattern of red insects on it—wasps.

'I don't know where you came from, but here it is considered very rude to mind talk in front others—especially in front of your queen.'

'You aren't my queen,' said Renee coldly, before Andy could say a word.

'Oh, I think you'll find you are mistaken on that point.'

Clio's eyes flashed a vicious red colour and suddenly Renee felt her hair slowly changing and her eyes. She looked like Rebecca Cole again. She felt her wings start to tingle.

'You can feel that too, can't you? The two of you are going to come with me or you are suddenly going to find yourself sprouting wings. That would be awkward, wouldn't it?' she said in a low threatening manner leaning forward across the table.

'Or someone is going to recognise you from your missing person's poster over there,' she said nodding towards the poster pasted to a light pole.

'So—what choice do you have?'

Renee desperately tried to thought talk to Andy, but she found it impossible, she could not change her features either. She suspected that Clio had somehow removed all of her powers.

'Okay. We'll go with you,' said Andy.

'Wise choice.'

Another woman appeared at the table. She was familiar to Renee somehow. She wondered if she was the fairy with pink wings that had seen her at the garage. Her hair was black, cut short and she seemed very wary of Renee.

'I want you to follow Gaia,' she said nodding towards the woman.

'I'll be right behind you, so don't try anything.'

Andy stood up and dropped some coins on the table for the coffees.

They followed Gaia down the street; conscious not only of Clio behind them, but also of a huge fairy escort hovering invisibly around them.

They followed her down a narrow alley and into an underground car park. It was empty.

Clio removed a small golden cage from her pocket. It looked like birdcage but would have only been suitable for a beetle. They had been shrunk and pushed inside it before either of them knew what was happening.

The cage was clipped to the belt around Clio's waist and they were suddenly smaller again as Clio and Gaia shrank and flew out of the car-park and into the light.

Renee closed her eyes. Being so small, the world was flashing past at an incredible speed. It was sickening and they were thrown from one side of the cage the other as Clio flew. Eventually they realised that their best chance of remaining in one piece was to lie flat on the base of the cage with one arm and one leg wrapped around the bars to stop them sliding or falling whenever Clio changed direction.

They were travelling extremely fast and Renee opened her eyes briefly from time to time to try to determine where they were. After about half an hour the last houses at the edge of the outer suburbs disappeared below them and they started the climb into the mountains. The bush was thick about them and they found themselves being thrown from side to side more often as Clio negotiated a path through the old gum trees. They moved deeper and deeper into a forest thick with eucalyptus trees.

They passed over gullies and rivers, over thickly wooded hills and into quiet shady valleys. At last they were so deep in the forest that there were no signs of man at all; no roads or paths of any kind.

A large gum tree almost two metres across at its base loomed before them. There was a large hole that pierced the tree completely, forming an archway through which they could see the forest beyond. They entered the hollow and instantly their view changed.

Before them were sprawling streets, some paved, some dirt. There were buildings made of wood, wattle and daub and mud brick. They had roofs made of wooden shingles, thatch or slate tiles. The largest and most imposing of these stood at the far end of the main road; the cobblestone paving merging into the steps at the foot of it. It was two stories high and the only building they could see that had been made from stone. There was a large wooden door sawn from the trunk of a single tree and it had a grey slate roof. There were two towers, one at either end of the large main building. It seemed to be trying awfully hard to look like an ancient English castle, but without really succeeding. The shape was too symmetrical, too planned, and the finish of the stone was rough and angular, the mortar messy as though a first-time builder had erected it. It looked amateur, like something you would find in a fun park.

They were taken into the castle. Clio returned to full size; Gaia following a second later.

The queen held the little cage up before her eyes.

'I have taken your powers away from you. In time, if you are deemed worthy, I may decide to return them to you.'

'Take them down to the dungeon,' she said passing the cage to Gaia. 'They can think about where their loyalties lie for a while.'

It seemed absurd that such a childish building could have a dungeon, but they were taken down a flight of stone steps into a dark basement room. True to form there was a small barred window high above them letting in some daylight and a heavy wooden door with a barred viewing hatch at eye-level.

Gaia placed the cage in the middle of the floor and then left the cell. She returned a moment later with a jug of water, a couple of cups and a loaf of bread. She released them from the cage and left the room, bolting the door behind her. She threw some powder at them through the bars in the door and they quickly returned to full size. She shut the hatch before they could say anything. They heard her footsteps going back up the stone steps. Their only light was that coming from the barred window.

This whole situation was ridiculous. She would have found it mildly amusing if she wasn't aware of what Clio was capable of. But the fact was, Clio was as big a monster as Bill. They were in real trouble.

Andy immediately tried to restart their thought conversation. He couldn't.

He moved as close to her as he could.

'They will be listening,' he said in a whisper close to her ear. 'I want you to see if you can return your wings to normal.'

She tried and to her surprise they returned to their normal size and shape. They were not their normal colour though; they were completely black–no hint of green at all and they were limp; she could not move them.

'Good. I thought that might be the case. We just need to wait,' he whispered.

When he saw that she was about to ask a question he put his finger to his lips.

Andy was looking around the room, and then she sensed them too. There was at least one fairy in the room somewhere.

The cell that they were in had two straw mattresses and an old tin bucket. She could guess what that was for. She wandered over to look at the window. It was too high up for her to touch, but she could see that the bars were made of brass. She looked over at the door and realised that all its fittings were either copper or brass too. There was no sign of iron anywhere. Were they only capable of primitive metal work?

Andy made himself as comfortable as possible on one of the mattresses, and she decided to follow his lead.

At some point they both fell asleep.

It was many hours later that Renee awoke. There was no light at all coming through the barred window, but the hatch in the door was open and there was some light entering the room through the bars of this. She guessed it was candle-light or a flaming torch as the light had a flickering quality to it. She looked over to Andy and realised that he was awake too. The presence that had been in the room was gone, but she could feel someone outside the door. Andy locked his thumbs together and made a bird shape with his hands, and then he pointed at her wings. In the dim light she could see that they had returned to their normal colour. He was smiling.

He reached out to her with a thought:

'Can you hear my thoughts now?'

'Yes! Have my powers come back?'

'Yes. She is an old fraud. She can take them away for a while, but she can't do it for long. Lucky she hasn't realised who I am or she would never have tried such a simple trick.'

'She knows you?'

'She did, a long time ago, before I became old and grey. Nancy and I had more than one run in with her, and we worked out some of her tricks. Don't do anything to give the game away. You have to pretend that you don't know you have your powers back. Pretend to be at her mercy. We can't communicate like this in front of her, or any of the other faeries, or they will know you have your powers back. It's really hard to thought-talk without appearing distracted.'

'Why don't we just escape now?'

'I want to know what she wants. What she is up to. If we know that we might be able to avoid any future run-ins with her.'

A noise outside broke off their conversation.

The door was opened and Gaia entered carrying a flaming torch. It hurt their eyes after the darkness of the cell.

'She wants to see you now,' she said and held the door open for them.

The passage and the stairs were lit by more torches and as they ascended the stairs they saw flickering torches and candles everywhere. They had no electricity.

Gaia led them along a hallway and into a large hall. Clio was seated on a gilded chair on a dais at the far end. There were chandeliers filled with candles and crystals throwing brilliant patterns of light and colour around the room. The floor was slate and the walls stone. There was a fireplace, cold and dark, to one side of the dais and she guessed that in winter the room would have been incredibly cold without it.

'You can leave now Gaia.'

Gaia bowed and moved back down the hall, closing the doors behind her at the far end of the room.

Renee could sense that Clio was the only fairy in the room, whatever she wanted to say, she wanted to say it in private.

'The ring you wear; this did not come from a queen,' she said to Renee. 'You have not sworn allegiance.'

'No. Nor will I.'

'I would not be so hasty if I were you. You will find life very hard here without your powers and life in the human world impossible, if you cannot disguise yourself.

'You are too dangerous to leave running around uncontrolled.'

So she knew about the incinerations, Renee thought, as she watched Clio pace up and down the room, her hands behind her back.

'The burning of the men in the garage cannot be explained by human science. You will bring attention to our kind. I do not want that to happen—not yet.'

So what does she want? thought Renee. Andy was staring at the floor, and she could tell that he was listening attentively, seeking to separate fact from fiction.

Clio spun around and stalked back towards them.

'Why did you want the human baby?'

Renee baulked. She had not expected this.

'Where did you come from? Is there a new gateway to the faerie realm?'

Renee remained silent.

'I will give your powers back to you if you swear allegiance to me. You must tell me everything and accept my ring to bind your oath.'

Renee stared at her. Clio wasn't one to mince words.

'And then what?' asked Andy.

Clio looked at him for the first time.

'Humans have no rights here. You will not address me at all. I allow you to stay for the moment because you have been useful to this faerie. You are old and weak, if I decide that your usefulness is at an end…'

Renee glared at her, 'This man is a father to me, do not threaten him!'

Clio watched her, imperial and cold.

'What will become of Andy if I agree to join you? And what are your plans for me?' Renee asked.

Renee suspected that Clio was not used to being challenged, especially by one that might be more powerful than her. She seemed to be struggling to hold her temper in check.

'If you behave, I will return your powers and you will both live long and productive lives in my realm.

'Here we are safe from the human barbarians. I have seen the monstrosities these creatures are capable of. The filth and violence of the second fleet was more than anyone could endure, and yet I survived while hundreds didn't! I vowed that we would never be associated with the creatures that created that depravity. We remain pure and untainted.

'They took our homelands away from us in Britain, with their railroads and factories belching smoke. They will not be allowed to do it a second time. In time we will destroy them and take back what is rightfully ours.'

She strode around the hall, suddenly agitated, excited. Extending her arms heavenward she turned to Renee, her eyes alight—'We will bring peace and justice to the world. Humans will be delegated to the lowest of the low where they belong. They are worthless savages, unworthy of the power they hold. We will reclaim what is ours, what has always been ours! And reconnect with our long lost sisters and brothers in the Emerald Isles. You will be my Memitim—my flaming sword.'

So she wanted to be judge, jury and executioner; how easy it was to fall back on that tired old solution. And Renee would be her flaming sword to carve the world to fit her carefully crafted shape of how things should be; a surgical instrument to remove the cancer.

War after war after war; bigger and better weapons, more and more death; lives and lands made barren and empty.

When had a megalomaniac's view of the world ever created anything but mass pain and suffering on all sides? How easy to think that in your hands the power would be different—better, purer—somehow; that all of that destruction would only come to those who deserved it.

The guilt hit her like a dodge ball in the stomach.

No.

No.

'No.' It was almost a whisper, but it felt like a shout.

'If you do not, you will be lower than slaves.' Clio was leaning forward now, her eyes glowing their true red colour.

Andy touched Renee's arm in warning.

She was not going to back down to this tyrant, but she wanted to know more.

'What is to stop me incinerating you as soon as you give me back my powers?'

Clio pulled herself upright and returned to imperial coldness. 'I'm not stupid—as much as you might wish it.'

She walked back to her throne and sat down. 'When you swear allegiance to me you will be bound to me; you will be unable to use your powers against me.'

'A ring,' Andy said quietly.

'I told you to be silent!' Clio snapped at him.

'Time to go. Quick!—before they realise,' he thought to Renee.

The queen rose from her chair her eyes flashing again.

'I have warned you once about your thought talk, there will be no second chance,' she raised her hands to strike him down, but Renee was too fast for her. She grabbed him around the waist and shrank them both to beetle size. They were off and out the window before the queen could even yell for her guards.

'They'll be on us in a minute', Andy thought to her while he desperately clung to her arm. They were heading for the entrance and passed through it just as it was sealed behind them. *'That was close—it won't hold them up for long. Head that way—can you feel the big old tree over the ridge?'*

'Yes. It feels wonderful! Like a warm hug.'

'That's Old Blue, the one I showed you in the memory. He is very old. He was a great friend to all the old ones who died in the faerie war. He will keep us safe if we can reach him before the others do.'

'When was the fairy war?'

'Ask me later, let's get safe first.'

The other fairies were coming up behind them fast.

'I'm slowing you down, I'm too heavy. You need to make me smaller, make me lighter. I'm going to grab hold of some of your hair, and then I want you to make me as small as your thumb. Okay, I've got a good grip, shrink me now!'

There was a sensation of pulling on her hair as his body shrank and his weight dragged on her hair. Once he was small enough, she could not feel his weight at all, and suddenly she found she could fly twice as fast. She started to pull away from their pursuers again.

She topped the ridge and started down the other side darting between the trees. The trees were thicker here and she could hear them racing up behind her as she slowed to dodge between them. They sounded like angry wasps.

She flew through a gap in the branches of a thick bush and darted sideways as she emerged to try and throw them off her trail. Some continued on, but others noticed her change in direction and kept coming.

She zipped between several trees that had grown twisted together and heard a thump as several of her pursuers crashed into each other in an attempt to follow her through the gap.

'Andy, are you still OK?'

'Don't worry about me, just keep going, we're almost there.'

Suddenly the enormous old gum tree was right in front of her, and she could feel it calling to her. She circled it and slipped inside a large knot hole under one of its branches.

She found herself inside the tree looking out. The tree had created an invisible barrier to prevent the others from entering; somehow it had sensed she was in danger. Renee watched as the other fairies zoomed past the tree oblivious to the fact that their quarry had vanished.

She bent double and tried to catch her breath. When she raised her head to look around she could see that the inside of the tree was surprisingly well lit. The wood was patterned and textured and the air was pleasantly warm.

'If they can sense me, why don't they realise I haven't gone any further?' she asked Andy, puffing.

'Ahh, that would be me,' said a strange soft voice.

Renee lifted Andy from her hair and returned him to her size.

'Hello, Old Blue!' said Andy.

'Andy! I must admit, I didn't think I would see you again. Is Nancy with you?'

'No... I'm afraid Nancy passed on some years back.'

'Oh Andy! I'm so sorry. She really was something special.'

'Aye, she was. But special faeries seem to be my fate—this is Renee. And a more special faerie I haven't met.'

Renee blushed; although it seemed absurd to be embarrassed in front of a tree, even if it was a talking tree.

'Renee, this is Old Blue, the same tree Nancy and I travelled to when we escaped from the lynch mob in Scotland all those years ago.'

'Pleased to meet you,' said Renee, feeling a little overwhelmed.

'The other faeries won't bother you here. They can't sense the doorway. I'm afraid they are losing their abilities with each generation and are starting to become quite savage,' said Old Blue.

'Yes, I think Clio is deliberately stopping them from using their powers. It's like an atrophy,' said Andy

'Why didn't they realise that the trail had stopped?' Renee asked the tree.

'I sent them on a wild goose chase,' the tree giggled. 'I bounced your aura off into the trees. It will fade to nothing eventually and they will wonder what happened.'

'My aura?'

'Yes, that's the part of you that they can sense. You can sense theirs too—it lets you know when they are near. It is your natural energy field.'

'How can you bounce and block my energy field?'

'Ahh well, you see, some faeries are tree spirits, and some are fire spirits, or earth, or air, or water. You are a tree spirit, so I can communicate with you and we can share some of our abilities—we are in harmony. More powerful faeries have more than one kindred spirit; yourself for example. You are a fire faerie too.'

'Am I?' she said surprised. And then a realisation took place. 'Yes, I suppose I am,' she said.

'That in itself is quite rare—trees and fire are not natural allies. But less of a conflict than say water and fire. That combination is extremely rare.'

'Do you know what sort of spirit Clio is?' asked Andy.

'I am afraid I don't know which one Clio is. They all seem the same to me, none of them are tree spirits. If you like, I can teach you to disguise your aura as a tree aura. That way none of them will be able to sense you and any other tree faeries will sense you as a faerie tree rather than a faerie.'

'None of these fairies would be able to trace me by my aura?' asked Renee hopefully.

'That's right.'

'Wow!'

'That would be good,' said Andy, 'we wouldn't have to worry about them trying to abduct you again.'

'What do I need to do?'

'I need you to put your hands on me; it doesn't matter where, and think about my aura, the things you could feel when you were flying towards me.'

Renee did as she was asked, and began to feel a warmth enter through her hands and into her mind.

'Can you hear me inside your head?' the tree thought-spoke to her.

'Yes!'

'Now I want to imagine that the warmth is surrounding you, from the tip of your wings to the tip of your toes.'

The strange comforting warmth rolled over her and clung to her like an invisible, but very comfortable second skin.

'As long as I am alive, this aura will stay with you. If you decide you want to remove it you can just imagine it sliding off, but only I will be able to restore it again.'

'So are there other things that I can share with you because I have an affinity with trees?' She spoke aloud so Andy could hear.

'You are already sharing some of your life force with me—not enough to cause you any harm, but because you are here with me I will grow well this year, better than in normal years. The most favoured faerie trees are the oldest and largest trees in any forest. It also means that I will not be troubled by any diseases this year. Your energy gives me a temporary barrier.

'You are a full-grown faerie, but I can tell that you are not the master of your powers yet. Once you are stronger, if you like, I can teach you to make a transporter; to seek out a tree in another location and form a new doorway.'

'Like the door Nancy and I travelled through from Scotland all those years ago?' Andy asked.

'Yes. It takes some time and a lot of energy to create a new door to a place as far away as that, but I can do it with the help of a powerful tree faerie.'

'Am I a powerful tree fairy?' asked Renee, bewildered.

'Oh yes! You just need a bit more practice.'

'You don't happen to know how I became a fairy do you?'

'I'm sorry—I don't know what you mean. You can't become a faerie. Either you are one, or you aren't.'

'I wasn't a fairy last year. I was a normal human; I didn't have wings, or magic.'

'I have never heard of such a thing,' said the tree in wonder. 'If that is true then you are a very special faerie indeed.'

'The others are heading back to the compound,' Andy said suddenly. Renee turned and looked out the entrance. Several fairies flew past; she could feel their frustration. A pink light stopped in front of the tree, circled it a couple of times, and then slowly moved away. It was Gaia.

'That one senses something at least. She is not as numb as her fellows,' the tree commented.

'Does she know I am here?' asked Renee.

'No. But she can sense that there is something different about me; that I am not an ordinary tree. It may be that her mother was a tree spirit. Sometimes, even though the child faerie is not a tree spirit themselves, a hint of ability can be inherited from a parent. She seems a bit more talented than the others, a bit more independent. I will keep an eye on her I think. I may be able to communicate with her in time.'

'I think it is time that we went home Old Blue. I can't thank you enough for your help,' said Andy.

'The pleasure has been all mine; why I can feel my girth expanding as we speak. It has been way too long since I sampled some faerie life-force. Please, come and visit whenever you like. Now, where can I drop you?' he asked.

Renee was confused again, but Andy soon made it clear.

'Have you got any doorways in Sydney anymore? Anywhere would do.'

'Let me see, I did have a door to old Kraken, but I closed that off, I discovered that he was poisoning me—can you believe it!'

'Actually I can,' said Andy.

'Oh there is another one in the botanical gardens, a lovely peppercorn tree called Pepper. Not very original, but it is rather appropriate. Going a bit senile I'm afraid. But I'm sure she would be up for a visit, assuming she isn't having a nap. Don't wake her if you can help it.'

'She would do nicely. If she's awake would you like me to pass on your regards?'

'Oh, yes please. I do need to catch up with her, but I always seem to catch her when she is napping. Her door is the old weathered one just there on your left.'

Renee walked over to an arch shape in the tree-wall. The pattern on the door-frame was of gnarled and twisted branches. At first, it didn't appear to be an opening at all, but when she looked closer, the inside of the frame seemed to wobble and flow, like a reflection on a lake.

'You'll need to hold my hand,' said Andy, 'I can't pass through by myself.'

'Goodbye Old Blue,' said Andy

'Thank you for everything,' said Renee.

'It's been lovely to catch up Andy, and it is always a pleasure to meet a fellow tree spirit my dear,' he said to Renee.

Renee took hold of Andy's hand and they stepped through the arch. The strange surface bent in wards as she pushed against it, and then for a moment it covered her like plastic wrap, before separating and wobbling back into an undulating surface behind her.

They found themselves inside another tree. This one was not as large as Old Blue, but she looked older. The inside of her trunk looked weathered and gnarly. There was a sense of peace and quiet inside. Renee could feel that she was gently sleeping. She laid her hand on the wood and felt the trees slow breathing. She also felt a small surge of energy pass from her hand into the tree. She felt the tree equivalent of a yawn and a stretch and then the tree "rolled over" and went back into a deep slumber. Renee smiled to herself; that might help a few aching branches.

'Which way?' Renee whispered, not wanting to disturb the tree any further.

Andy pointed to an arch to their right. There were images of a lawn and flowering trees outside. They quietly stepped through.

The sun was brilliant and the sky a deep clear blue.

They breathed a sigh of relief. Not far home now. They were still beetle size.

'Do you want to ride in my hair again?' asked Renee.

'Sure—why not. Save my aching legs a bit.'

Renee shrank him and he jumped onto her hand. Once he was safely settled in her hair she flew home.

Tom was sitting on a stool with his elbows on the table while George sat on the opposite side preparing to open up the files on the USB stick.

'What's to stop it infecting the whole network with a malicious virus?' Tom asked.

'Standalone computer. No Internet connection.' He opened up the file manager and clicked on the stick.

'Anything?'

'It's encrypted. I have a code breaker on here, then I'll do a virus scan.'

'I'm in—,' George said a few minutes later, '—and it's blank.'

'Shit.'

'We have got one more chance. His home computer had an external cloud account. If I can crack into that…'

'How long will that take?'

'How long is a piece of string…?'

'Right.'

'It's a legitimate cloud service. I already have a warrant to cover it, but they are being a bit slow giving us access. I'll call you if we get in.'

Tom nodded, and wandered out.

Since the physical evidence wasn't much help, he decided to find out what Mr. Bill Doyle was up to. Peter had been keeping an eye on him, so he went up to his office to see if there had been any progress.

Peter wasn't there. He went inside anyway and closed the door. He pulled out his mobile. Peter answered after the second ring.

'Any news on our suspect?'

'The last couple of days he's been at work all day; keeping his head down. But he finally went out today and I got some nice footage of him slipping supplies to a couple of known runners. Not enough to act on yet, but a nice start. There is one other thing. He went for a walk down around the waterfront at lunch time and made small talk with a young runaway, a girl. Got the video; too far away for audio unfortunately. She's taken over Babayaga's old nest.'

'I've got a couple of beat cops giving me a hand; I think we'd better keep an eye on her. Keep her safe.'

'Yeah. I think he was playing Good Samaritan today, but who knows how long that will last.'

'I'll see if I can get approval to put in a surveillance camera nearby. Get the boys to position it when she's out and about.'

'I'm gunna head off home now.'

'Thanks Pete, I'll get the uniforms onto her tonight.'

He hung up the phone and went off to find Gardiner and Peale. Hopefully one of them would be available for an extra shift tonight. Otherwise he would have to do it himself.

Clio stood in the centre of the throne room, her hands clasped tightly behind her, lost in thought.

Gaia knocked twice on the side of the open door and the queen turned to face her.

'Well?' she said impatiently.

'No sign your majesty. She has vanished.'

The queen frowned and waved her away.

Clio did not even know the faerie's name—that was a severe oversight. It was un-queenly and ill thought. A name was power. The more you knew about your enemies the more power you had over them, and a name would have opened many possibilities. Or a hair.

She snapped her fingers, 'Gaia!'

Gaia returned.

'While they were sleeping; did you take one of her hairs?'

Gaia started. 'No, your majesty, I did not know you wanted one.'

The queen sighed. None of the current guards had been fighters in the faerie wars. They did not have the instinctive survival skills or the forethought that fighting in a war instilled. A warrior from the old days would have known to take a hair; to take any advantage (honourable or otherwise) as a means of overpowering a dangerous foe.

She should have ordered it as soon as they were captured. Was she slipping?

'Never mind,' she said. 'Go. Go!' she barked shooing her out.

So, the guards could not find her; she had hidden herself somehow. Unless of course Gaia did not want to find her…

She suddenly looked to the door. Suspicion was second nature; it had kept her alive all these years, through the war and all the minor uprisings since.

No.

Gaia had always been loyal; she had never questioned an order—not so much as a raised eyebrow.

This new faerie knew some tricks. Perhaps they were tricks from the old country? Perhaps they were tricks from another country. She had heard of djinis, brownies, and selkies with their own magicks. Perhaps this faerie had knowledge of their ways.

There was one thing that she was going to have to nip in the bud. This faerie knew that the paralysing spell was temporary. She was able to wait it out and escape. That had never happened before. If Clio's subjects found out that she could not take their magick from them forever there would be a revolt. If they started thinking for themselves…

Time for another fairy story.

'Gaia! Summon the swarm.'

Constables Gardiner and Peale had been on rotation in an unmarked car watching the girl 24/7. Gardiner had been awesome; luring the girl to a cafe for a talk and a meal, and although she hadn't been able to get her name or age, it had given the surveillance team enough time to get a hidden camera in position. They could now record every meeting with Bill. And there had been a few.

The girl was in desperate straits and was too naive to realise he was grooming her. Over the last few days the gifts of food and money (as well as the sympathetic conversation) were slowly winning her over. She now smiled when she saw him coming.

They hadn't been able to identify her, but suspected she was sixteen or seventeen years old; probably a runaway from some kind of care. She was extremely wary of authority, so they knew better than to approach her and ask her about Bill.

So far, Bill had done nothing illegal. No grog, no drugs, just food and cash. Until he slipped up, they couldn't do a thing. All they could do was watch.

Clio took her time preparing herself. She needed to look powerful and all knowing. A long black gown of velvet tightly fitted in the bodice and increasing in fullness until it cascaded to the floor in decadent folds. An intricate pattern of red wasps adorned the throat and wrists; from a distance their arrangement was reminiscent of dripping blood.

The mood must be set. She would wait until darkness had fallen and the torches were lit. She would wait until the swarm were nervous with anticipation, then she would appear above them in her magnificence. She would be a strong virtuous ruler using her strength to keep her people safe from the power of the evil interloper; one queen against another. Just as the queen bee must fight off a challenger, so must she to protect her swarm.

She strode out on to the steps at the front of the palace.

'My people!' she cried, raising her arms. She waited a moment for the noise to subside. 'We are in deadly peril. A queen from another swarm has come among us.' She waited again for the noise to die down before she continued. 'But do not be afraid, for this interloper is not as strong as I, and she will not succeed in her quest to destroy us!'

She held herself regally erect imagining the crowd exploding into cheers. The reality was somewhat different; a sea of murmurings and mutterings. There were no jubilant faces, ready to fight to the death. Her people were worn and tired. They had been waiting for her for hours.

She pushed ahead, knowing that they needed change; a challenge to unite them under her glorious leadership.

'She came here to threaten us, to tell us that she would take what is ours. She is no lone faerie, but the queen of another swarm, come from the old lands to force us out of our safe haven. Have I not told you time and time again that the old lands are dying under the weight of iron; that our kind are dying in droves! Have I not told you that someday, they may find us here in our sanctuary and try to steal what is ours? Well here is your answer! They are on our doorstep!

'I have consulted the old writings and our records of magick and I have discovered how she was able to escape me. The queen has drained the very power from her entire swarm to be able to escape from us, to make herself invisible to us! Her whole swarm will be weak for days. This greedy queen has milked her own people dry to save herself!'

There were a few of those amongst the crowd who drank in her every word, excitement and wonder in their eyes; there were the young who looked anxious and fretful; then there were the old ones who viewed her with hard eyes and hearts. She was oblivious to all but her adorers.

'I shall seek her out while she is weak and show her my power. She shall not come here again unless it is in iron chains! The old human she calls father—he shall carry my message to her.'

She turned to face Gaia, 'Gaia, my faithful servant, you shall be the one to take the message to her,' Gaia moved forward and knelt before her. Clio passed her a wooden box, its open lid revealing a jagged dagger.

'You shall hunt the old man and bring me his heart in this box,' and then taking a hair from her own head she wove a filigree ring of gold with a single wasp at its centre.

'You shall put this ring on his finger. Then she will know that I can take from her whatever I wish to take, and she shall receive nothing that is mine unless I wish it to be so.

'Rise and go to your task.'

Gaia stood, bowed once and flew off into the forest.

'Soon, all of you will celebrate my victory over the invading queen!' And with a flounce of velvet she spun on her heel and disappeared into the palace.

The adorers wandered off in awe. The young turned to the old. The old tried to comfort them, but knew that trouble of some kind would come to them soon.

Gaia took the box and flew to the clearing by the river and waited.

Half an hour passed before the queen appeared before her.

'This time the orders are to be followed as given. No deception. Kill the old man and bring me his heart. I have left a message in this ring for the faerie. Place it in his dead hand.'

'Where would be the best place to start my search your Majesty?'

'You have seen her more than I, go to all the places where you have found her and then search the area around the cafe where we captured them. If you get too close she will sense you, so try to find the old man alone. He should be an easy kill.'

'Are we prepared for war your Majesty?' said Gaia anxiously.

'There will be no war. He is the source of her power. She is no queen, and she has no swarm. It is he that provides her with her inner strength. Once he is dead, her power will be gone.'

Gaia bowed once and flew off into the trees.

Gaia

Gaia flew deep into the trees until she came to the mighty old gum tree where she had last seen the faerie. It was bigger by far than any other; it was as thick as a house and taller than the palace. She walked around it once, and then again. There was nothing to see that was not completely ordinary, yet something told her that this tree was more than it appeared; there was a tiny ache in her heart.

'Old tree, can you speak to me?' she asked it.

There was no reply.

She placed her hand on the smooth mottled bark, but pulled it back immediately when she felt a strange pulse. Delicately she placed her hand back on the tree.

'Old tree, can you hear me.'

'Yes my dear, so nice to meet you at last. I have seen you flit about and wondered if you might come and speak to me one day. I am Old Blue.'

'You call yourself "Old". Most creatures fear being called old.'

'For a tree, "old" is the greatest of compliments. Grey bark is a sign of wisdom, experience and the sign of a healthy life well lived.'

Gaia stared at the tree in wonder. 'Are all the trees as sentient as you?'

'No. Some have never been, and some were once, but sleep deeply now. I can communicate with some of the trees, but I am one of only a few who can still talk to faeries.'

'Why do they sleep?'

'Without tree faerie magick, we can only last so long; the slumber overtakes us. There have been so few tree faeries here at any time. Now, there are almost none.'

'How is it you are not sleeping?'

'Where a normal faerie tree might converse with a faerie once every couple of years, I was bathed in faerie magick almost daily for a hundred years. It has sustained me.'

'Do you fear that one day you will fade?'

'I do not want to fade; but I am old. If it comes, it comes.'

Gaia was suddenly aware that she was asking questions of the tree that were rather personal, but that the tree did not seem to mind in the least. There was something about the tree; it felt like they had known each other all their lives.

'I'm sorry, my name is Gaia. I hope you do not feel like I have been interrogating you.'

'Not at all; it is too long since I last spoke to a faerie. To be honest, I must apologise to you, because, without even consciously thinking it, I have been happy to keep you talking. You see, I absorb power from you.' Gaia jumped back for a moment, losing connection with the tree.

She looked at her hands, and mentally checked herself over; she did not feel weakened. The tree was her best means of finding the faerie, and she hoped it hadn't be offended by her reaction—she couldn't really help it. She placed her hands back on the bark.

'Sorry about that,' she said sheepishly, 'I wasn't expecting that.'

'Not to worry. Perhaps I could have broken that to you a little better. I won't hurt you or weaken you. However, I would suggest giving old Kraken a wide berth if you ever come across him—he is a nasty old relic. He has the ability and the depravity to kill the golden goose.'

'Kraken! How strange; I used to know a Kraken...' Gaia didn't understand the goose reference, but made herself a mental note to find out about it.

'Do you know where the other faerie went? The new one?'

'Ah. Well, I don't know if I should answer that.'

'The old man is in grave danger. I need to warn them.'

'Clio has sent you —yes?'

'She has given me one task; I am choosing to perform another.'

'Ahh—a rebel!'

'Shhh. Not so loud. That word means death here.'

'Don't worry, my dear, haven't you noticed that your lips are not moving? Neither one of us is speaking aloud.' Gaia was momentarily startled.

'How did I not realise that?'

'One of your parents was a tree faerie would be my guess, and you have the abilities without knowing it.'

'Surely they would have told me?' she asked silently.

'In Clio's realm, perhaps not. There are many reasons for many secrets here. It is safer to appear ignorant. Clio herself lost her parents too young to know many of the things that she should.'

Gaia wondered about this for a moment, and realised it was a basic tenant of existence in Clio's world. Knowing more than the queen could get you killed. She addressed the strange old tree again.

'Will you help me get a message to them?'

'First you will have to make me a promise.'

'What kind of promise?'

'That you will not hurt Andy or Renee or knowingly do something that will cause them harm.'

'I can do that. I have no intention of harming them.'

'This is not a promise to make lightly, it is binding, and I will know if you break it.'

'Some kind of tree magick?'

'Yes. Very old tree magick.'

'I promise I will not harm the faerie and the old man, Andy and Renee, nor deliberately do something that will harm them.'

'You have promised; I will keep you to that promise. I can't talk to them directly. Not unless they are here with me, but I can take you to Old Pepper. She might be able to help.'

'How can you take me anywhere?'

'I am a doorway. Above your head, under my branch, there is a knothole. Do you see it?'

'Yes, I see it.'

'Make yourself smaller and fly up inside.'

She briefly wondered if she was a gullible fool about to be consumed by a sweet tongued tree; a fly about to be ensnared in a Venus fly trap. She threw her doubts to one side and plunged into the knot hole.

Inside was a strange warm world of wood; amazing textures and light. The chamber was roughly cylindrical, tapering to a point at the highest part of the roof. Ridged and patterned areas decorated the sides, and there were three archways outlined by curving gnarled branches. One of these was bordered by oak branches and looked old and grey; the wood within the arch was charred black. One was surrounded by smooth sinuous branches but the wood in the centre looked green and mouldy. The last was bordered by the twisted knobbly branches of a peppercorn tree. Within this arch the wood seemed to wobble and distort like a reflection in a pool of water.

The whole room was dimly lit by a warm glow emanating from the wood.

'If ever you need refuge, you are welcome here,' the old tree told her.

'Some faeries grew tired of the battles that waged between faerie and human (or faerie and faerie for that matter) and entered the trees. Some of them chose to stay and in time they and the tree became one—the Greeks called them dryads.'

Gaia got the feeling that the tree would be happy to impart all sorts of knowledge to her; that perhaps he didn't get to chat very often.

'Do you get lonely Old Blue?'

'More often than I used to, I am afraid. Old friends have gone and tree faeries are few and far between these days.'

'Once I have completed my task; may I come back and talk to you some more? I know nothing of tree faeries.'

'That would be wonderful,' the old tree replied with emotion. 'But first,' the tree continued, pulling itself back together, 'there is work to be done. Let me see if Old Pepper is awake.'

A low hum vibrated through the tree and the surface of the peppercorn arch began to vibrate in sonic ripples.

'Yes, she is awake—well she is now anyway,' the old tree laughed.

'Visitor to see you, Pepper. Give her any help you can please,' the tree spoke to an unseen entity.

'Through the doorway, Gaia, and you will find yourself in Pepper's lobby. She might be able to send out a call for Renee and Andy, but you may have to wait a while for a response.'

'Thank you so much, Old Blue. Will I be able to come back this way again?'

'Oh yes. The doorway between Pepper and I is old and stable, I will look forward to our next chat.'

'Thanks again,' she said and pushed slowly through the wobbling surface, passing through a vast distance in an instant.

Old Pepper was an elderly peppercorn tree with attitude. Too old to care about the opinions of others, she was eccentric, but endearing.

'Hello young'un, where have you sprung from? Haven't seen a tree faerie in decades; although Blue Boy keeps telling me I slept through one visit, lying hussy that he is,' she said with a chuckle. Gaia had the distinct impression that Pepper would have winked at her if she could.

'I didn't know I had any tree faerie in me until today. I didn't know there was such a thing.'

'Yes, there weren't many tree faeries sent over in the first fleet, or the second one for that matter. Most of them were able to head for the trees when the humans started meddling in faerie lands. It was the other kinds that got caught and sent over in the ships. Iron manacles—nasty, nasty business. So how did you end up here young miss?'

'I live in queen Clio's realm—'

'Oh! Can't help bad luck I suppose—'

'I was just a child when I came over on the First Fleet with my parents. My parents thought the new world would be safer than England,' she shrugged, 'turns out they were wrong.'

'There is always hope, pixie; times change. Clio can't live forever.'

'I need to talk to a faerie who lives somewhere near you. Are you able to summon her for me?'

'I can try. But I haven't felt any faeries in my region for a very long time.'

'She hasn't been here long. I don't know where she came from, but she is definitely a tree faerie.'

'Well, that will make it easier. Let me see…'

Freedom

It had been almost a week since they started watching the girl. She was still safe, but Bill had been to see her once or twice every day. Surely he would make a move soon?

The longer this went on, the bigger the risk that someone on surveillance would get complacent and slip up. Then she could be in real danger.

There were still no leads on who the girl was. She did not match any New South Wales missing person's reports so they were starting to go through the interstate reports now.

Bill was starting to get very familiar with her. If it turned out she was underage, they may be able to get him on grooming charges, especially if he started to give her alcohol.

Every day the danger to the girl increased. If Bill didn't make a move soon, he would go and speak to her. Try to convince her that Bill was bad news and help her get access community services. He couldn't let this go on for much longer.

Gaia stayed with Old Pepper for two days. The call to Renee and Andy was a low, vibrating hum. It continued day and night (when Pepper wasn't sleeping). The old tree liked to nap, so during these times Gaia would leave her in peace and scout about the area, searching for Renee or gathering food.

She visited all the areas that she had seen her; the garage and the café in particular.

Towards the end of the second day she emerged from the tree and quickly changed into human form; she needed to stretch her legs. She turned around to find Renee standing there. Gaia jumped her heart racing. She could see Renee, but could not sense her presence.

'How is it that I cannot sense you?' she asked Renee.

'Old Blue helped me. If you stop trying to sense a fairy and try to sense a fairy tree instead…'

Gaia looked at her curiously, and then concentrated on Old Pepper. Yes, there was awareness that the old tree was something special. She looked to Renee, and had the same, vague feeling.

Renee continued, 'I came here last night, while you were away. I spoke to Old Pepper and Old Blue. Old Blue tells me that I have nothing to fear from you, that you made a binding promise to him.'

'Yes. I will not cause you harm. Clio—unfortunately—she has other ideas. She is afraid of you, and if you won't join her, she will try to punish you.

'But I don't understand—where did you come from? There have been no new faeries in this country in almost a century, not since the wooden ships stopped coming.'

'I can't answer that question yet. I don't know the answer myself,' Renee said. She wanted to be able to trust this fairy, to have another of her own kind to talk to freely would be an immense relief, but she would limit what she told her for the moment.

'Why do you stay with Clio, when she is such a monster?' Renee asked.

'It has not been a matter of choice. I am protecting others. Being close to Clio's side is the best way to know what she is planning. I was caught out once before, people I cared about were hurt, and I will not allow that to happen again. Clio is completely oblivious to the pain she has caused me, she would not trust me if she realised that she had wronged me, so I trust you will keep that information to yourself.'

If that was true, Gaia was prepared to go out on a limb for her. Then what did she want? Was this just a ploy to win her over, or was she sincere?

'Yes. You can trust me. I have no battle with you. If Clio keeps pushing me though, I may not be able to say the same for her.'

'I came here to warn you. She has ordered me to kill Andy—'

Renee flinched.

'—which I will *not* do!' Gaia finished hurriedly raising her hands and taking a step backwards. 'I have no fight with either of you.'

'What does she want?'

'She has ordered me to kill him and place his heart in this box,' Gaia said holding up an ornately carved wooden casket.

'Oh my god; Clio is channelling the evil queen from Snow White?' Renee exclaimed.

'I have no desire to face Clio's wrath when I return empty handed,' Gaia added.

'So we place an animal heart in the box instead,' Renee finished.

'How did you know that was what I was thinking?' Gaia asked, puzzled.

'Snow White is a very old fairy tale that humans tell, perhaps you have heard bits of it somewhere?'

'Yes. A long time ago someone told me a story…' Gaia was lost in thought for a moment.

Renee's sixth sense was at work again. She was sure that Gaia was not a danger to her, just as Andy wasn't. Clio on the other hand was something different. Her instincts had told her that Clio was cold and dangerous right from the start. Renee was willing to trust Gaia to a point, and for now, that was enough. She wondered if Gaia felt the same impulse of trust, of connection, or if it was it one of her own unique abilities.

'I can go to the butchers and buy a sheep's heart. I'm sure between the two of us we'll be able to make it look more human.' Renee told her.

'There is a shop that sells hearts?'

'Yes; for pet food mostly.'

'Oh,' said Gaia, wrinkling her nose in disgust. 'Please, lead the way…'

As they walked, a sudden impulse struck Gaia—

'By any chance, is there a fairy tale about a golden goose?'

George was sitting at his bench, Mr. Layton's computer set up in front of him. He had cracked the password days ago, but was only now getting around to backing up the entire file system to an external hard drive. Once he'd done a full security scan, Tom could go through the contents at his leisure.

Five, four, three, two, one, done; the little green bar hit 100%. George stretched, his back cracking; he had been sitting too long again.

Now for the fun part, he thought.

Loading the password cracking tool had been the easy part. Now he needed to break into the guy's external cloud storage. He had an independent mobile data connection already set up, secure and separate from the main police communication system. He didn't want any nasties infecting the mainframe.

He opened up the password screen for the cloud service and set the password breaker running; time for a cup of tea.

Ten minutes later he returned; it was still running.

He went back to his plaster cast work.

An hour later he realised what time it was and went over to check on its progress.

Done. He was in.

Unfortunately, the guy also had a secondary encryption system set up.

Bugger. This might take weeks.

He checked the password Layton had used for the cloud service.

How could this guy be so smart and so dumb at the same time?

Cloud123.

He tried Encrypt123, then Encryption123, and finally the brand name of the encryption tool with 123.

The last worked.

After a quick look at the files and he was smiling more than he had in weeks.

Tom was going to be beside himself.

Renee called to Andy with her mind and told him all she had learnt from the trees. He met them at the peppercorn tree and Renee shrank him and carried him inside. It was a safe, neutral place for all of them and their presence gave Pepper some much needed life force. Old Pepper was dozing. Andy trusted the trees implicitly, but he was still a little wary of Gaia. It made him grumpy and standoffish.

The sheep's heart had been neatly placed in the wooden casket. A simple transformation spell performed by Gaia had made it appear less ovine.

'All this subterfuge raises some issues,' Andy grumbled at Gaia. 'How are you tied to Clio—what spells has she placed on that ring of yours?'

Gaia held up her hand, the filigree ring twinkling in the tree-light.

'Does she force all of you to take a ring from her?' Renee asked.

'No. And yes.' Gaia replied. 'Without the ring, the younger faeries cannot disguise themselves as humans. They are mostly half-bloods and do not have the powers that we full bloods have. My case is different; I made a choice to take the ring. During the faerie war, my parents were suspected of being sympathetic to the rebels. I had to prove my allegiance to save them; I accepted the ring. I am bound to Clio, I cannot harm her, but I have read the words of the spell carefully—it says nothing about having to obey her,' she said in triumph.

'How did you obtain the exact words of the spell?' Andy asked in wonder.

'It is an old trick my mother taught me. Do you have a small piece of paper?' Andy passed her an old receipt from his wallet. She wrapped it around the ring and blew one long breath on it. When she unwrapped it, written in tiny cursive writing were the words of the spell. She passed it to Andy.

'Well I'll be damned,' Andy exclaimed, squinting at the tiny writing. He took out his reading glasses and examined it closely.

'Would that work with my ring?' Renee asked Andy, 'there were no words, just ideas.'

'Never know until you try…'

Andy handed her another docket and Renee wrapped it around her ring and gently blew across its surface. When she unwrapped it, it was covered in tiny pictures, each representing an idea; each clearly identifiable to her, although Andy had some trouble interpreting them.

Andy passed Renee the paper from Gaia's ring, but she could not read the words, they were all in the language of the Sidhe.

'What does it actually say?' she asked him.

'Well, not much actually. I am guessing you got this ring a long time ago? Before she perfected her technique?' He asked, gazing over the top of his glasses at Gaia.

'Yes, mine was one of the first created.'

'Well, it says is that while you wear this ring, you are bound to Clio, and can cause her no harm and tell her no lies. It also says Clio has the ability to remove your powers forever should you ever remove it—which is a load of old cods wallop by the way—no one can do that. She can numb you for a while, shock you into powerlessness, but it doesn't last for long.'

'So Gaia can remove the ring now…'

'Hang on; hang on, not so fast. If you remove this ring, Clio is going to know and you won't be able to thought talk with her anymore.'

'What if I had another ring made from Clio's hair?'

'It would depend. Do you know what spells are on the other ring?'

Gaia held out the ring Clio had made for her mission. 'This was to be placed in your hand, once I had killed you.'

She wrapped a third piece of paper around it and blew gently.

'This one is no good,' Gaia said. 'All it has is a message, to be relayed when it is touched by Renee,' and she passed the paper to Andy.

'"Anything you have—I can take from you. Obey me or face the consequences. I await your return." Nice sentiments. Noble and Queenly,' said Andy scowling. 'Hang on to it. We may find a use for it in time, but no good for now.'

'I do have something else...' said Gaia, holding out a vial containing two or three dark hairs. 'I thought they might be useful someday.'

'Heh heh heh,' Andy chuckled. 'Well done. This could be very interesting.' Renee could see that his opinion of Gaia was rising by the minute.

'You can use another fairy's hair to make a ring?' Renee asked indignantly.

'It's not as easy as using your own and there are some things you can't do, but this is old magick. Hair of the dog, voodoo; all kinds of cultures use hair or personal belongings to target their curses and spells,' Andy explained.

'Do all of those things exist too?' Renee asked incredulously.

'Not all. But a lot of them are based on magicks that are real.'

'We should be able to use one of the hairs to create a ring for Gaia that will communicate with Clio, but not have all the other nasties attached to it,' he explained.

'Is that what you want...?' Renee asked Gaia, 'to be free of her?'

'Yes. But she mustn't know yet. There are things I need to do first.'

'Are there others who feel the same way? Who want to be free of her?' Andy asked.

'Yes; but how many I don't know. Any sign of treason is dealt with in the most terrible ways. Most are afraid to say anything to anyone. There are a few rebels hiding in the trees, but their numbers are small; not enough to make a difference. Not yet.'

'So, the war didn't wipe the fight out of you completely. Good to hear.'

'When was the war?' Renee asked, feeling a little like the dunce in the class.

'It ended in 1983. It started way back when Clio came to power— must have been a hundred years before that,' Andy said.

'How do you know so much about our history, our lore? Are you a part blood?' Gaia exclaimed.

'No, no... I am the husband of a faerie. My wife and I visited Clio many years ago and I have some very old bones to pick with her. So I warn you now, do not cross me,' he said looking her in the eyes over the rims of his glasses. 'Clio will not know what hit her when I get my chance.'

Renee had never heard him talk with such ferocity.

Gaia did not appear troubled by his words. If anything, she looked inspired.

Gaia continued—'I cannot lose her trust yet. I am in her inner circle. I think that staying there, for the time being, will be of benefit to both of us. If I take this ring off—will she feel it? Will she know?'

'I can't be sure. If you were dead—yes she would know; if you have only taken it off—I don't know.'

'What if we make a new ring first?' Renee asked, 'put it on before we take the old ring off?'

Andy looked at Renee thoughtfully. She really did push all the boundaries. But then, he supposed, she had never learnt what the boundaries were.

'That might work. At worst, Clio would feel a bit of a blip when the old ring comes off. But what if she gets suspicious—does she know the trick to reveal a ring's spell?'

'Not that I know of; my mother told me never to reveal any of my spells to Clio and I don't think it is widely known. Our most powerful magick died with the rebels in the war.'

'If she feels a blip, she will want to talk to you straight away. You may not be able to if your powers are drained. She might get anxious. How will you explain it?'

'That I have just killed you and escaped Renee. That Renee tried to put a spell on me, but it only clipped me. It drained my powers for a while.'

'Ok. That sounds plausible. One problem; she might see me wandering around. However, once upon a time a faerie put a spell on someone I know so that I could never see or hear them again—they became invisible to me, and I to them. Do you know how to do that spell?'

'Yes. It is the outcast spell. Sometimes a faerie is banished from the colony...'

Renee's eyes widened as the implication of Gaia's words hit home. A fairy banished from her own kind, never to see or hear them again; left to hide among humans or wander alone forever. What a terrible existence; and yet so close to her own in so many ways.

'I need you to banish me from Clio's view. She must be sure that I am dead. But I still need to be able to see and hear her.'

'That I can do.'

'Another ring?' Renee asked and Gaia nodded. 'I think you are running out of fingers Andy!'

The two rings on his fingers were small, but another would start to look conspicuous.

'Can a new twist be added to one of your existing rings?' Renee asked him.

'How do you mean...'

'Weave the hair through the filigree on one of your current rings.'

Andy looked at Gaia. 'What do you think?'

'I don't know. If they join together, you might have to take them both off at once. Maybe you couldn't separate them again. Taking one off would lose everything from both rings.'

'Both of my rings are made so they can come on and off without unwinding.'

'You can do that?' asked Gaia surprised.

'Oh yes. We can do that when we make your new ring if you like.'

'So do you think the new hair would just fall off if the ring it was taken off?' Renee asked.

'All we can do is try...' Andy was a little predictable at times. She found it oddly comforting. 'When you say the spell, add a condition that the hair will remain a ring when it is removed, but that the two rings can be pulled apart.'

Andy held out his hand and as Gaia spoke the words of the spell she wove one of Clio's hairs into the ring that Renee had made for him. She had to repeat the words over and over several times before the hair would obey. Eventually the hair and the ring became like liquid gold, entangling their patterns to form a single ring. The metal became solid again; a slight variation in the colour of the gold distinguishing the old from the new. The ring was only slightly larger than the original, but more intricately patterned. Gaia wrapped a piece of paper around the ring and blew gently.

'Looks like it worked,' she said as she passed the paper to Andy.

'Yes. It looks good. Let's see what happens when I take it off,' he said as he slid the ring off his finger. The ring glowed slightly but remained whole. He plucked at the new part and it unwound itself, coiling again into a separate ring. He held the two rings out for them to see.

'Wow,' said Gaia, 'I didn't really believe that could happen,' she said looking at Andy in surprise.

'What happens when you put them both on again?' Renee asked; childlike in her curiosity.

Andy slid the first ring onto his finger, and then the second. As soon as the second ring came in contact with the first, they twisted themselves together again.

'That was way too cool,' Renee exclaimed staring at the ring on Andy's finger. 'Do it again, dad, do it again!'

Andy laughed, Gaia looked confused.

'You really are her father?' she asked him.

'Adoptive father; of sorts,' he smiled. 'Now it's your turn... You will be safe here with Old Pepper if you lose your powers. You may not get them back for a day or so.'

'Yes. She will keep me safe.' Gaia replied, patting the tree gently. It was like she had been an orphan all her life, and now she had found a loving aunt and a raft of other welcoming relatives. Her link to the trees felt so natural, so fulfilling, she wondered why it she had not noticed it earlier.

'Aren't you tired? Renee asked, breaking Gaia from her thoughts.

'No. Not at all. This kind of magic has never drained me.'

'Will Clio notice if the ring is on a different finger?' Renee asked.

'Probably; but I think I can slide this one down a bit,' and she wiggled her existing ring until it was sitting just past her knuckle out of the way. She wrapped another of Clio's hairs around the base of her finger and said the words of the communication spell. Again, it did not happen the first time. She had to concentrate hard and continue to chant the spell time and time again before the hair behaved. The new ring was very similar to the old. It was unlikely that anyone would notice the difference.

'Okay, taking off the old ring will be the real test.'

Gaia held her breath and slid the old ring the rest of the way off her finger. Instantly it reverted to a long dark hair, Gaia's wings drooped, lying flat against her back and becoming a dull grey colour; her eyes lost their sparkle.

'How do you feel?'

'Drained; but I didn't notice any kind of pulse. I don't think Clio is aware.'

'Well. That's good. But stick to the story anyway. She may try to contact you while you are weak. She'll get suspicious if you don't mention that you were unreachable next time you talk to her.'

'So what do we do now?' Gaia asked.

'Wait to see how long you are out of action. With Renee it was about twelve hours. I will be interested to see if it is the same for you.' He settled himself into a comfortable niche in the wall of the tree and stretched out his legs.

'Did you learn all this from your faerie wife?' Gaia asked Andy, settling herself onto a bench-like protuberance.

'A lot of it. And from her mother. But I had been conversing with faeries since I was little.'

'Not here, in the colony?'

'No. In the old country; Scotland.'

'Where you born in the colony?' Renee asked Gaia.

'No. I was born in England. My parents and I stowed away with the convicts on the first fleet. One of my uncles was a convict; he was caught trying to destroy the ironworks that was being built in our valley. He was in chains; in pain and completely powerless. My parents and I accompanied him to ease his pain and make sure he survived. We thought we might have a better life in the new colony, away from the iron factories and railroads that were springing up everywhere.'

'You came with the first fleet?' asked Renee.

'Yes.'

'Before Clio?'

'Yes. Things were very different here before she arrived.'

'Was there another queen then?' asked Andy.

'No. We were just a bunch of faeries living together and trying to survive. We had no idea how hard it would be. We really didn't think that the English would just send the convicts off to die on a foreign shore, but they did. Or they had absolutely no idea what they were doing. Everyone on the ship thought it would be a land of plenty. I remember seeing the shore for the first time, the haze from the eucalyptus trees gave the whole place a blue tinge. The glare and the light on the water and the sand, it was all so strange; so wild and beautiful and empty. But it didn't t take long for us to realise we were in trouble.'

'Did no one have the skills to survive here?'

'Some did, but there were too many that didn't; the convicts had been stuck down in the hold for most of the five months it took us to sail here, they were pale and weak from lack of sun and exercise, and before that, a lot of them had been imprisoned for years in the rotting hulks in the Thames. Many were too sick for hard labour. Food was very scarce. Stealing food was punishable by death. The soil was thin and sandy; nothing would grow. The trees were as hard as rock, almost impossible to cut—oh! I hope Old Pepper didn't hear that!—drought and theft left us all close to starvation at times. We faeries dared not reveal ourselves, and we lived in miniature to conserve energy and reduce our food intake. We tried to help—to make the plants and animals thrive, but nothing was the same here. Even the grasses were different. We were just as lost as the convicts. Eventually, we made friends with some of the local aborigines and left the convicts to their own devices. In return for food we helped the Iora people with their injuries. The foods they ate were very strange to us, but eventually we got accustomed to it and we started to make our own little village in the hills; but the second fleet—that changed everything.'

'Why? Because of Clio?'

'Partly. Clio's father, King Rory was the ruler of the entire English swarm. He was captured in human form and sentenced to transportation for life for his part in the fight against the mills and factories. He was chained for the entire journey. Clio and her older brother went with him in faerie form to try and help him. One third of the convicts died on the way over. King Rory was one of them. They threw his body overboard like a common thief. It was a terrible desecration. There was no king's funeral, no ceremony to guide him to the land of the dead, no passing of the crown. When the ship landed, the faeries were ready for war, but thankfully, Prince Reagan managed to calm things down.'

'What happened to Reagan?' asked Andy, 'I've never heard of him.'

'He was made King, and for a while, we had peace; but Clio would not forget, nor forgive the humans. She started to make trouble. Convicts, officers, settlers they were all the same to her—all worthless humans. Even the Iora, the aborigines, that had helped us survive in this wilderness for two years were not spared. She thought they were beneath us and she tried to enslave them. They stopped helping us. We nearly died of starvation. Clio fought with her brother, she wanted to conquer the Sydney settlement and take their food, but her brother knew that the food would not last long, and unless we learnt from them and established our own farms we would be in trouble again. He wanted to make secret treaties with the farmers; use their superstition to our benefit. Establish a new folklore where we could swap healing for food and live together in peace.'

'It sounds ideal. Obviously it didn't happen. Clio, I assume?' asked Renee.

'Yes. We had an altar; a shrine, near a waterfall. It was all going so well...'

Gaia stopped. She pulled her legs up until she was sitting cross legged on the bench and rested her elbow on one knee, her chin resting in her palm.

'It lasted almost a hundred years. Then she killed him and took the throne.'

'What? She killed her own brother!' said Renee

'Yes.'

'Why wasn't there a rebellion?'

'There was. The hundred years war.'

'Ah. So that's how that got started,' Andy said. 'I never knew that bit.'

They sat in silence for a while, considering what they had learnt, and then Renee said, 'I don't understand one thing. Before, when you were talking about your uncle and then later the king, you said they were captured by humans and they were powerless to escape. Why were they powerless—why couldn't they just shrink and fly away?'

'Because of the iron,' Gaia answered puzzled.

'Iron?' Renee asked, looking at Andy for assistance.

'Yes… I had noticed that about you,' he said taking off his glasses and putting them in his pocket. 'Iron doesn't bother you at all does it?'

'No… Why would it?'

'Normal, run of the mill faeries can't stand the stuff. Weakens them; makes them completely powerless if they are chained in it—and it burns like hell. But I have seen you run your hand along iron railings without even wincing,' Andy said.

'Did Nancy hate iron?'

'Like the devil. You may not have noticed but I ripped off all the iron lacework on the outside of my house and replaced it with wooden fretwork. Took me ages to do that. There are no iron pots, no iron beds; I even painted the iron gas heater in the bathroom with about an inch of heat resistant paint.'

'Have you ever met another fairy that could touch iron?'

'No.'

'What about you Gaia?'

'No.'

'Oh…'

The Beginning of the End

Renee and Andy returned to the tree the next morning with a basket of breakfast for Gaia. They had expected her to regain her powers during the night.

'Still no good?' asked Andy looking at her pale wings and lacklustre eyes.

'No. I hope it comes back soon. Clio will have been trying to contact me.'

'Stick to the story, and you'll be fine. It won't be much longer I am sure,' he said, but his eyes told another story when he glanced at Renee.

'What are your plans when you head back?' asked Renee.

'Nothing initially; I want to make sure that Clio is satisfied that everything is back to normal before I take any risks. Once I am sure the ring is working properly, and Clio is not suspicious, I will go and seek out the rebels. I need to find out how many there are and what they want; whether they are willing to try to free the others, or if they have given up on revolution. Do we leave Clio and her followers to their fate and join the rebels, or do we try to depose her? I don't know. It is not my decision to make; I need to consult the others.'

It was late in the afternoon before Gaia regained her strength. Her wings and her eyes regained their vibrant pink colour and she felt back to normal.

'I need to get back to Clio. Thank you for all your help.'

'Thank you for not killing me,' said Andy. 'One day, when things settle down, I might ask you to help me find a faerie. Someone I haven't seen for a long time.'

'Of course, I'd be glad to help.'

'Do you think Clio will leave me alone after this?' asked Renee.

'I don't know. I will tell her that I never got to speak to you, and that I killed Andy after tracking him down at the cafe. Maybe she will think she has achieved victory over you, maybe she will send me back to hunt you, who knows? She is completely mad. I will warn you, somehow, if she decides to make trouble for you again.'

'I would offer you a ring to communicate with us, but I think that would be dangerous for you,' said Renee

'Yes. Clio would demand to know where it came from; who I was consulting with. She is paranoid enough already.'

'Good luck Gaia. I am sure Old Pepper will be happy to send out another call if you need us. She is looking almost sprightly with all the faerie essence she has been absorbing,' said Andy.

It was true; Old Pepper had a glow to her timber; a warmth and smoothness that had been missing before.

'I feel quite sprightly for such a daft old biddy,' the tree chided.

'Sorry Old Pepper, I thought you were asleep,' said Andy.

'Not to worry. Make sure you don't stay away too long, I am quite enjoying my spruce up.'

'Wouldn't that be a pepper-up?'

'I'm not specie-ist, dear. We all return to dust one day.'

They made their farewells to Gaia and Old Pepper and flew home.

5:00 PM; knock-off time for Bill. He had been in the habit of dropping past the girl on his way home. Today was no different. At five twenty, Tom made a note of his arrival and turned up the volume on the monitor.

'Still here?' crackled out of the speakers.

'Yeah. Haven't had any better offers,' she said. She was smiling.

'Well, I've got a sandwich for you,' he said removing a wrapped bundle from his pocket and passing it to her, 'and an opportunity, if you're up for it.'

Tom watched her take the sandwich and begin wolfing it down. Either she was very hungry, or she was afraid he might take it away again. He noticed her glance to the other side; checking the exit was clear? Perhaps she wasn't as naive as he had thought.

She finished her mouthful, 'what sort of opportunity? I told you, I'm no pro.'

'Nothing like that; I know the guy who runs a grocery shop near my place. He needs a bit of help in the shop. He can't pay much, but there is an old flat above the shop that he uses for storage. He said he can clear a corner of that for you to sleep in. It's not flash, but it's safe and warm and it has a bathroom.'

'How old is this guy?'

'He's seventy in the shade.'

'Is he married? Kids?'

'Yep, two grown up kids, and grandkids—real family guy.'

Tom watched her; she seemed to be weighing up the offer.

'I'm not saying yes and I'm not saying no. Not until I meet him.'

'Fair enough; but you're gunna have to get cleaned up first—I don't mean to be rude—but you pong.'

She laughed. 'No shit. You try living like this one day. The bathroom is a shocker.'

'Never mind; my sister and I are sharing a house a few doors down from the shop. You can come and get cleaned up and then I can take you to meet him. Sue's probably got some spare clothes that will fit you too. Sound good?'

'Is your sister home?'

'Yeah. She only works mornings.'

Liar, Tom thought. Bill had no sisters.

'All right then. But it's just a meeting OK—I'm not making any promises.'

'Deal.'

She grabbed her valuables and followed him walking up the road to his car.

'Shit,' Tom swore. Peale and Gardiner weren't back from their break yet.

'Gardiner?' he spoke into the police radio.

'What's up boss?'

'She's on the move, are you in the car?'

'Just heading back now.'

'I'll update you once I see where they're heading.'

'OK, out.'

Tom waited until she had climbed into the passenger seat of Bill's car before he slipped his own car into gear and pulled out of his parking space. Tom was in a nondescript white sedan, one of thousands driving around the city every day. Bill pulled out into the traffic and Tom followed; two or three cars between them.

'We're in the car, where are you?' The radio erupted into life, it was Peale's voice.

'Heading south down Elizabeth Street into Redfern. He's in a dark blue Holden Commodore; New South Wales rego plates SLU 150. Just passing Cleveland Street now.'

'OK, we're on the move, we're heading south down Devonshire Street, should be in sight of you soon.'

'He's turning right into Redfern Street, I'm three cars back. He's gone left into Pitt Street, there's only one car between us now.

'We can see you.'

'Traffic is thinning out, he's turning again—stay on Pitt Street if you can, I'll follow him into Turner Street.'

'Gardiner is going to do some laps.'

'OK. He's just pulled into a driveway, there's an alley along the side—I'm going to try to get a look. Come and park somewhere on Turner Street in case he comes out fast.'

'Will do.'

Tom parked and walked back to the alleyway, turning on the mini camera attached to his collar. The lane ran down the side of the house that Bill and the girl had just entered. There was a trellis on the top of the fence covered in climbing plants and Tom was able to see the front of the house and the narrow garden running down the side from his position.

He turned the volume on his police radio to low and inserted the ear-piece.

'They've just gone inside,' he whispered, 'can you hear me?'

'Yep. We're fifty metres up the road from you; just parking now.'

Tom turned, spotted them and gave them the thumbs up.

'We ran a check on the car; it's registered to Bill Doyle.'

'What? He's using his own car?'

'Yeah. Bold as bloody brass.'

'If this goes bad, it could go real bad real quick. I suspect he'll dump the car and run.'

He heard a shower start in the house and wondered how far Bill was going to take the ruse.

Ten minutes later the shower stopped. He heard muffled voices and then nothing for another ten minutes. The front door opened and he saw Bill carrying the girl to his car. She was unconscious; or dead.

'He's carrying the girl to the car; I can't tell if she's alive or dead. Shit. He put her in the boot. He might be taking her to his home base, follow him, but don't let him see you, we'll alternate the tail. Radio for backup. Over.'

'Got that, we're ready to go.'

Tom slipped back up the alley to his car.

When Andy and Renee arrived back at the house, they found Bruce on the veranda waiting for them. He was pacing backwards and forwards and chewing on his finger nails.

'Where the hell have you two been?' he demanded.

'What's up?' asked Andy.

'Inside—can't talk here,' he said.

Andy unlocked the door and Bruce hurried into the kitchen, and then continued his restless pacing.

'The young girl, the one who took over Babayaga's patch. She's gone.'

'Do you know where?'

'Bill.'

'Are you sure?'

'Yep; reliable source.'

'Shit.'

'When?'

'An hour ago, maybe more. She got into his car and they drove off.'

'We've got to tell Tom,' said Renee

'The cop?' asked Bruce

'Yeah.'

'Can you trust him?'

'As much as anybody,' said Andy pulling his mobile phone out of his pocket and speed-dialling Tom's number.

'Voice mail. Shit!'

He drummed his fingers on the kitchen table.

'I can take him a note. I'll go to the police station,' said Renee

'It's dangerous—you can't let the other coppers see you.'

'No. I'll stay out of sight. I'll find a way.'

Bruce grabbed an old envelope out of the recycling bin, and tore the back off it. He scrawled a note on the back while Andy looked over his shoulder.

'That do?'

'Yep. That'll do it.'

Bruce passed it to Renee and she shrank and disappeared out the window.

'Be careful!' Andy called out, but she had already gone.

'Tom, we're heading North up Chalmers street, just passed Wells Street,' Peale radioed in.

'Got that, I'm on Pitt Street, I'm going to cut across in front of you and pull in behind him.'

Peale kept an eye out for Tom while Gardiner drove, following Bill at a distance.

'OK, we see you; we're four cars behind you. We'll turn right into Cleveland Street and then head north along Crown Street,' Peale said.

'He's still heading north. Shit, a marked police car has just joined us. He's a couple of cars in front of me, and right behind Bill. Let's hope Bill doesn't get spooked,' said Tom.

'We're caught in traffic, there's been a dingle, looks like you're on your own for a while,' radioed Peale.

'Understood; he's turning right into Albion St. The marked car is turning with us.'

'Roger, we'll try and get clear of this mess and catch up.' Peale turned on the police lights hidden in the front grill of the car and turned on the siren. Gardiner started to weave her way through the backed-up traffic as the other drivers squeezed up to make way.

Bill's car began to shake violently; cars around him started laying on their horns.

'Something's going on; Bill's car is rocking around, I think sleeping beauty might be awake.' Tom said, 'I'm going to move into the bus lane to get a better look.

'Shit, she's kicked one of the rear tail lights out. Her foot is hanging out the back of the car. The uniforms have just put their siren on.'

'We're still trying to get free of the traffic,' Peale said.

Bill accelerated fiercely and made a wild turn to the left.

'He's running—left turn into Crown Street.'

The marked police car ahead of Tom accelerated and moved into the bus lane in front of him, its tyres squealing as it made the left-hand turn, hard on Bill's tail. Tom followed, keeping back a little. The police car swerved sharply to the right to avoid a bus stopped in the bus lane in front of him, and Tom followed suit, a riot of horns protesting in his wake. He continued to keep back, hoping Bill wouldn't notice him.

Bill swerved in and out of cars, moving to the wrong side of the road to dodge another bus and then careening back again. Cars were acknowledging the siren on the marked car, pulling to the side of the road to let the police car through; oblivious to Tom, they were hampering his progress. At the last minute, Bill swung his car to the right, taking the corner on two wheels. The police car overshot the turn and disappeared down the road.

Tom took the turn, driving sedately, waiting to see where he would go next.

'I'm on Burton Street, the marked car has overshot the turn, it's just him and me now. He's slowing down, turning left into Womerah. Where are you?'

'We've just got past the jam, heading north along Crown; we'll be with you soon.'

'He's turning into Oswald lane, I think he's gunna do a runner. Yep, he's dumped the car and is on foot—heading for the footbridge. Get the girl out, I'm going after him on foot.'

'Roger that.'

Renee flew straight to the police station and entered the building through a loose roof tile and a ceiling vent. She made her way directly to his office and was disappointed to find he wasn't there.

She zoomed back out into the open plan area, keeping an ear out for any word of him. There were plenty of officers at work, but there was little conversation. She wondered where else to look.

Peter! He was on the floor below. She slipped into an air vent and followed the ducting to the floor below. The dust was cloying, and thankfully she was so small that her coughing and spluttering was too quiet to be heard.

Peter was in his office, but no Tom.

She was wondering what to do next when a door opened further along the hall and she recognised the distinct tone of a police dispatcher before it drifted closed again. There was a gap under the door and she slipped inside. Several police officers sat at computers, headphones and microphones in place, giving instructions and information to the police on the line.

'What's your position Constable Peale?'

'We are heading into Burton Street. Request an ambulance to meet us in Oswald Lane, one female, trapped in a car boot, possibly injured.'

'Roger that, will dispatch.'

'DI Hayes is pursuing a suspect on foot, heading over the William Street footbridge towards Bayswater road, needs immediate backup. We are at the car. Out'

'Acknowledged,' the dispatcher changed frequencies. 'All cars in the vicinity of Bayswater road, Rushcutters Bay, officer needs assistance.'

Renee didn't wait to hear more, she slipped out of the building, heading for Bayswater Road.

Bill was already heading off across the footbridge when Tom pulled up behind his car. Bill looked back, startled to see someone coming after him, and picked up his pace.

Tom could hear the girl screaming blue murder from the trunk of the car.

'Calm down, the police are on their way,' he yelled as he passed it.

He was half way across the footbridge when his radio beeped. He slipped the ear piece into his ear and turned the miniature video camera back on.

'Tom, we're at the car, what's your position?'

'In pursuit, crossing William Street on the footbridge now, need my breath to run.'

'Roger.'

He increased his pace, his long legs cutting the distance to shreds. After a couple of glances, Bill was not bothering to look back any more. Bill was out-paced and he knew it, the question was, did he have any other tricks up his sleeve. Was he was armed?

The footbridge was a long one, crossing seven lanes of traffic, and the car fumes rising up from below were tearing at his lungs. Bill shot off the end of the bridge and turned abruptly at the bottom, doubling back along Bayswater Road.

The sun was setting, if he didn't catch him soon, he could easily slip away into one of the lane ways or back alleys in the darkness. Tom upped his pace again, closing the distance between them.

Bill ran along a side street and ducked into the trees lining an oval. Tom lost sight of him for a moment among the shadows but caught sight of him again as he darted past one of the picnic tables near a gazebo containing outdoor barbecue facilities.

As Tom passed the table, Bill stopped, turned and fired.

Tom felt an enormous pressure collide with him, a searing pain tearing into his chest. The blast knocked him backwards, his legs buckling underneath him. He lay sprawled, gasping for breath and he saw Bill walk slowly towards him, gun raised, a crooked smile on his twisted face.

'Doesn't pay to be fast; better to be a plodder don't you think?' he said as he walked towards him.

It was dark now. There was no one about.

Tom felt the dry grass pushing against the back of his neck. Where had the bastard pulled the gun from? Why hadn't he seen it?

Bill moved closer, gun aimed at Tom's chest.

'I love killing coppers; almost as much as killing whores. I like to do my little bit for the community,' his laugh was harsh and manic.

'Thought you had me, didn't you? Looks like you're done for mate; that was a really nice shot. Seems a waste to use another bullet, but I like to be sure,' he smiled again and raised the pistol to Tom's head.

Tom knew that he was going to die. He felt oddly calm.

A green light caught his attention. A Christmas Beetle. Always bloody Christmas beetles.

And then the world exploded.

Bill awoke in the back of a police paddy van. His arms and legs were cable tied.

He lolled from side to side as the van turned corners.

When at last it stopped he heard a viewing port slide open.

'He's awake.'

'Let's get him out, the doctor's waiting to see him.'

For a moment he was confused. Was he at the nursing home?

Then the back door of the van opened and two policemen stood in front of him.

'We can do this the hard way, or the easy way. Which is it gunna be?'

'Easy,' he muttered.

The two officers grabbed him by the legs and dragged him to the edge of the van.

'Any trouble and Don will Taser you—understand?'

'Yes.'

The policeman cut the cable ties on his legs and helped him to his feet.

They marched him over to the entrance to the police cells.

The large metal door opened with a groan.

The end is nigh.

Not long after the explosion, Peale and Gardiner arrived on the scene with reinforcements. They bundled Bill into a paddy van and a short time later the ambulance arrived to take Tom to the hospital. At least that's what Peale had told him; he didn't remember any of it.

Tom had minor cuts and head injuries from an exploding gas bottle. Peale told him that it looked like Bill had shot it by accident. His ears were still ringing. He had thought he had been shot, but obviously not—although his shirt would seem to indicate otherwise. The doctors said his memory would come back in time.

Renee was exhausted. Andy's warnings about killing herself trying to cure someone of cancer came back to her with renewed clarity. How close had she come? Tom's injuries had been terrible. Once she had started, she hadn't been able to stop herself. She couldn't have left him half cured could she?

Well, really, she could have. She could have healed him to the point where he wouldn't die and then left. She needed to start thinking a bit more and not just reacting to things. She needed to start putting her own health and safety first.

She had drained herself so badly she had been unable to speak to him. She had put herself into a dangerous position. What if Tom had tried to catch her—she would have been powerless to get away from him.

Well now it was time to rest. She didn't feel up to telling Andy about this, not yet. If she turned up at home like this he was sure to guess that something had happened. She knew a quiet place to rest for a while, but first she needed to speak to Andy. She created a thought connection.

'Andy, the girl is safe and Tom has arrested Bill.'

'Fantastic! Do you think he's got enough on him?'

'Yes. If he can't get him put away for this, then he is untouchable.'

'Good work. We should celebrate.'

'Maybe another time, Andy, I am not really feeling like it tonight. I am going to go and see my baby.'

'Ahh. OK... with Bill in gaol, it's finally over isn't it?'

'Yes. It's over...

...I just don't know what I am going to do now.'

'*Well, there are plenty of options, but you need some time to process this first. No need to rush into anything.*'

'*No.*'

'*Once you have had some time out, there is something I might get you to help me with.*'

'*Busting more drug dealers?*' she laughed.

'*Well, there's always time for a bit of that, but no, I was thinking of something a bit closer to home. Something I've been meaning to follow up for a long time. But it could be dangerous.*'

'*Sounds interesting.*'

'*Goodo. Don't stay away too long.*'

'*No. I won't. I'll see you soon.*'

She broke the connection.

Time to rest.

Tom was sitting at home in front of his easel, trying to decide if his latest painting was finished or not. He didn't want to overwork it, but he wasn't satisfied with what he had done. As he scanned the ripples of paint a blowfly trapped in the window buzzed impotently against the glass.

Bloody flies and bugs.

And Christmas beetles.

The miniature video camera on his collar had been destroyed in the gas explosion. But he had an automatic backup to the cloud...

He dropped his paint brush on the floor, splattering paint all over the place and hurried to his computer.

He had been having the strangest dreams; incredibly real and incredibly impossible. His hands were shaking as he opened the video file.

It was intact. He had been afraid it might have corrupted. He fast forwarded to the moment where he caught up with Bill.

He saw the gun fire and the whole world tilt as he collapsed, he could hear his own heavy breathing and groans of pain.

'Doesn't pay to be fast; better to be a plodder don't you think?' he heard Bill say, but he was still out of the range of the camera.

Bill entered the frame, moving closer, a gun aimed at Tom's chest.

'I love killing coppers; almost as much as killing whores. I like to do my little bit for the community.' He was laughing.

'Thought you had me, didn't you? Looks like you're done for mate; that was a nice shot. Seems a waste to use another bullet, but I like to be sure,' he was smiling as he raised the pistol to Tom's head.

Tom felt his stomach turn and his skin prickle as goose bumps broke out all over his arms. He remembered this moment. He had known that he was going to die; the odd sensation of calm acceptance.

It was then that a brilliant Christmas beetle had appeared. The camera caught it as it flittered behind Bill, unnaturally bright. Then the picture went white, a blinding flash; the gas bottle behind Bill exploding. But Bill had been pointing the gun at him...

The recording continued, the whiteness subsided and Bill was no longer standing over him. He could not see where Bill was. He could hear his own voice distorted with pain, screaming for help. There was a strange green glow in the video, and a tall glowing woman moved into view.

She was breath-taking. Tall and slender with dark red hair and incredible dark green wings that were shot with black silken patterns. Her entire body was emanating a soft green glow, and her wings had a jagged, wild look about them. She looked like some kind of a faerie daemon, but she had the face of an angel. Her eyes... her eyes were like shimmering green opals. She knelt before him and he realised he was remembering everything that he was seeing on the recording. His dreams had not been dreams; they had been memories.

She had gently taken his hand, lifting it from his bloody chest wound and placing it on her forehead and holding it there. Her other hand had reached down and closed his eyes; he had thought at the time that she was performing some kind of last rite for him. He had sobbed.

Then he had seen through her eyes—and gasped. He opened his eyes and lost the vision, and she had gently reached forward and closed them again. He could see what she was seeing—see her looking down at his bloody shirt. His chest had been torn open and the blood was flowing down his side. He could see bone and flesh.

She opened his shirt, gently pulling it away from the wound, and when he saw the extent of the wound, he knew without a doubt that he was dying. She placed her hand over the wound and suddenly the vision changed, they were entering the wound, plunging down into the bloody hole. He could see the shattered bone, his pumping heart nicked by the bullet; haemorrhaging and struggling to beat. Further in they went, down to his back; to his spine and the back of his ribcage. There was the bullet, lodged in a shattered rib bone. He felt a strange tingling and saw the bullet vibrate and wriggle free of its cage. It floated out and the bones reformed behind it, meshing back together and sliding back into place. Then they were reversing, sliding backwards out of the wound, and as they went, the bullet came with them and the muscle reformed, the blood returned; a backwards stream filling the arteries that writhed like snakes as they re-joined and closed.

The tingling continued as they passed his heart, blood streaming into its chambers and the pulsing muscle reforming and returning to a steady beat. More bone and muscle, flesh and veins, returned to their normal state, and then they were outside his body and the last of his skin was undulating and meshing.

She took his hand from her forehead and he opened his eyes. A smear of his blood painted her forehead like a ritual marking. Her hands were red.

He was alive. He was whole. He tried to say thank you, but his mouth gaped like a fish, and nothing would come out.

She placed a finger to her lips and gently shook her head. Then she took the camera from his collar and destroyed it.

The recording finished, but he hadn't been watching it anyway; he didn't need it to remind him anymore.

She had looked tired and drained, her glow had dimmed, and her wings were drooping. It had obviously cost her something to do this for him.

He had felt tired and weak, but he was alive.

Then the sirens had come. She had stood and smiled a tired smile. Then she had disappeared before his eyes, a tiny spark, a Christmas beetle, flying off into the night.

He had sat up, running his hand over the non-existent wound. The night had become chilly and he had pulled his shirt around him. It was tattered and covered in blood. Bill was lying a few feet away, unconscious or dead. He hadn't really cared which. He had got up and gone over to him. Bill was alive; and so was he. He had pulled a couple of cable ties from his pocket (much more compact than hand cuffs) and bound Bills hands and feet.

That was when the police officers had turned up and the ambulance had been called.

He was alive.

He had been saved by a Fae creature.

She landed next to the rock marking the grave and lay down in the soft ferns surrounding it. The burbling of the waterfall was a calming sound.

'It's over James. They won't be able to do this to anyone else.'

She ran her hand over the smooth stone.

Such a little life; a short and painful life.

'We have our revenge James. Why do I feel so empty? I thought this would end it, that we would be free now.'

She had cried so many silent tears alone in her bed. She felt incapable of crying any more at the moment.

'I will stay here tonight my darling, but tomorrow I have to try and find a future that includes me. I need to work out what I am going to do next. I may not be back for a long time. But I will come back when I am stronger. I will always come back. I will never forget you.'

Tom was back at work and Bill was safely behind bars. His bail application had been denied.

The girl was safe, and community services were helping her get her life back together. It would take time. She was willing to testify and there was enough video evidence and police testimony to back her up.

The question was, was Bill the Stonefish? Or was he just another slimy toady?

Actually, there were thousands of questions.

Were the rumours about an underground lair true; were any other girls in trouble? How many people were involved in all this?

And what was the creature that had just saved his life—and more importantly, what did she want in return?

He suspected that the old man knew more.

He didn't have time for this now.

He had to concentrate on closing Bill's horrendous crime ring down, and that meant doing the hard yards, wading through the mass of information that George had been able to pull off Layton's computer. Mr Jeff Layton did not trust Bill Doyle at all—that much was very clear. Every dollar spent, every shipment provided, every two bit hustle, all documented in obsessive detail. Layton had more than enough to blackmail Doyle if necessary. The trouble was the sheer volume of the stuff. It was like wading through mud in search of a diamond.

He already had enough to put the wind up Bill, but he needed more if he was going to get him for the murder of Rebecca Cole as well.

There was a photo of her on his desk; a constant reminder of the real once-living person that he was doing this for.

It was surprising how similar her face was to that of the Fae woman…

The room was brightly lit and devoid of all furniture except for a small table and three plastic chairs. Bill was slouching in one of them, arms crossed, staring at the wall. A uniformed police officer was sitting opposite him adjusting the settings on the interview recorder. There was a camera mounted in the corner of the room and a two-way mirror in one wall.

The door opened and he glanced up when Tom walked in and visibly started.

'I thought I'd killed you, you prick.'

'Don't suppose you've got that on have you?' Tom asked Gardiner.

'No unfortunately.' She pressed the record button as Tom took his seat. 'Interview with Bill Leonard Doyle commencing at 3:45 PM Monday 21st December. Detective Inspector Thomas Hayes and Constable Lia Gardiner in attendance,' she said.

'How well do you know Mr Jeff Layton?' asked Tom.

'Never heard of him.'

'Well that's odd, because he knows all about you,' he said, pushing some papers across the table to him. 'Do you often get strangers depositing money into your bank account?'

'I can't help it if some homo stalker wants a piece of me.'

'Well, where you're going everyone is going to want a piece of you—get used to it.'

'You got nothing. Where is my lawyer?'

'We rang Mr Hewson; he was not inclined to come. Would you like us to contact another lawyer for you?'

Bill was flustered, surprised.

'It will save us all time and money if you just tell us where the other girls are,' Tom continued, 'We know you were involved in the murder of Rebecca Cole, and I have a list of other offences as long as my arm.

'You are done, mate. Do yourself a favour; I can probably get the prosecutor to go easy on you if you tell me what I want to know,' Tom said.

'Piss off. You've got nothing. No deal. I want to talk to my lawyer, *Mr Hewson*, in private.'

'Constable Gardiner, could you arrange a phone for Mr Doyle, please? Interview suspended at 3:52 PM,' he said and switched off the recorder.

'I wouldn't bother spending too much a on a lawyer, Bill. With all the evidence we have, it wouldn't be a worthwhile investment.' Tom smiled at him and left the room.

Epilogue

Bill was sitting at the interview table again; Constable Gardiner guided Mr Hewson in and left, locking the door behind her.

'Nice of you to turn up—*finally*. This place is probably bugged.'

The lawyer pressed a button on his watch; a red light flashed and then went green.

'If it is, it's super high tech. I think we can speak freely.'

'Did Johnny give you that?'

'Yes; best of the best. It has come in handy.'

'What the fuck is going on?'

'I spoke to your accountant yesterday. Your fighting fund is empty. I am not a pro bono lawyer. Unless you can give me proof that you can fund a very expensive defence case, I am not interested.'

'What? Where has the money gone?'

'The funds have been annexed by your business associate. The police have confiscated all your other assets as part of their investigation—since they were potentially purchased with the proceeds of crime.'

'Don't worry about the money. I will speak to Johnny,' said Bill.

'Well, once you have, then we can discuss your defence.' He got up and knocked on the door. The Constable opened it for him and allowed him to exit the room.

'I need to make another phone call,' Bill said standing up.

'"Please" always helps,' she said and closed the door in his face.

The muffled curse that followed brought a smile to Gardiner's face.

An hour later, Bill was escorted to a prisoner phone.

Once he was alone he quickly dialled a memorised number.

'What the hell is going on? Where is my money?'

'No; my money. I have taken back my half of the proceeds plus the money you owe me. You got into this; you get yourself out of it. The doctor and I have a lot of work to do. You've made quite a mess.'

'If you hang me out to dry I will crucify your ass.'

'Now seeing you achieve *that* would almost be worth it.'

Click.

Bill swore under his breath. He had one more chance. He quickly dialled another number. He would have to risk it; the call was probably being monitored.

'It's Bill. I have another job for you. I need the papers.'

'How are you going to pay me from gaol?'

'Not a problem. If this works big bucks for both of us, if not, I have another option. When have I ever let you down?'

'The first time will be the last time man. The usual place.'

'Yeah. Be discrete—the boss man doesn't need to know about this.'

'Good as done.'

'I'll ring you tomorrow.'

The following day Bill queued for the phone again.

'You have them?'

'Yes.'

'Good. I'll get back to you later today.'

He hung up and dialled again. The prisoner behind him started grumbling.

He gave him the finger, 'Shut the fuck up, I've got twelve minutes.'

The phone was answered by a secretary, and he changed his tone. 'Could I speak to Mr Cole please? Tell him it's Bill; an old school friend.'

There was a click followed by elevator music.

The phone clicked again.

'I've been trying to call you for weeks! Where the hell are you?'

'Yes. Not very smart are you. This line is not secure by the way,' said Bill.

'What?! What the fuck?'

'I need you to come and visit me. Long Bay Gaol.'

'What?! Are you insane?'

'Old school mates should stick together you know, through thick and thin. And the way things are going it could get very thin for you. You don't want me to spell it out do you? You know some people who can help me. I need an introduction. So come in and say hi. NOW.'

Click.

ABOUT THE AUTHOR

Rhonda Selg was raised in a small town on the east coast of Australia.
She liked to write and paint from an early age and dreamed of becoming an artist. After school she moved to Canberra to study graphic design and then fell into a routine day job; following her creative pursuits in her spare time.
She lives in Australia with her husband, children and pet chooks.

Filigree Rings and other Fae Things is the first novel in her Filigree and Fire urban fantasy series and is set in modern day Australia.
There are three more books planned.

You can find out more about her upcoming books or subscribe to her mailing list at http://www.rmselg.com.

www.ingramcontent.com/pod-product-compliance
Lightning Source LLC
Chambersburg PA
CBHW021429110726
47901CB00008B/2352